South Side Sports

Discard

First and Ten

Jeff Rud

ORCA BOOK PUBLISHERS

Library and Archives Canada Cataloguing in Publication

Rud, Jeff, 1960-
First and ten / Jeff Rud.
(South Side sports ; #3)

ISBN 978-1-55143-690-6

I. Title. II. Series: Rud, Jeff, 1960- . South Side sports ; #3
PS8635.U32F57 2007   jC813'.6   C2006-907052-0

Summary: Matt is trying to make the football team while getting
to know his long-absent father.

First published in the United States, 2007
Library of Congress Control Number: 2006940597

Orca Book Publishers gratefully acknowledges the support for
its publishing programs provided by the following agencies: the
Government of Canada through the Book Publishing Industry
Development Program and the Canada Council for the Arts and the
Province of British Columbia through the BC Arts Council
and the Book Publishing Tax Credit.

Cover design: John van der Woude
Cover photography: Getty Images

Orca Book Publishers   Orca Book Publishers
PO Box 5626, Stn B.   PO Box 468
Victoria, BC Canada   Custer, WA USA
V8R 6S4   98240-0468

www.orcabook.com
Printed and bound in Canada.

010 09 08 07 • 4 3 2 1

For my brothers, Barry, Tim and Mike,
and their families.
JR

Acknowledgments

The author would like to thank Orca publisher Bob Tyrrell for his continued support of the South Side Sports Series, as well as Orca associate publisher and editor Andrew Wooldridge for his keen eye and sound judgment. The author would also like to thank Lana, Maggie and Matt for providing their love, support and plenty of peace and quiet.

chapter one

His thighs ached, his lungs burned for oxygen and his entire body was coated in sweat. Lined up with fifty other huffing kids wearing shoulder pads, white midriff jerseys, shorts, helmets and cleats, Matthew Hill tried to raise his own knees as high as Coach Reynolds was demanding from his spot on the grass ten feet in front of the players.

"Come on, you guys! Drive up those legs," the coach shouted as he raised his clipboard toward the cloudless blue sky. It was four o'clock, and the hottest part of the afternoon had already passed, but it was still uncomfortably humid.

Mid-August was normally the time when Matt would be playing hoops at Anderson Park or swimming out at Long Lake. But this year was different. This year, he had decided to go out for middle-school football. And football, Matt was quickly discovering, was not a sport for wimps.

"Okay, bring it in," Coach Reynolds ordered. The boys trying out for the South Side Middle School varsity team seemed to groan collectively as they gathered in front of the coach, some gasping for air with their hands planted on their thighs. After a couple of months of summer holidays, this was a rude awakening for everybody.

Matt thought he had kept himself in decent shape over the summer. It hadn't been that long since baseball season ended, and he had been playing pickup hoops at Anderson on an almost nightly basis. But this was a different kind of workout. He was finding Coach Rick Reynolds, a short, balding man in his mid-fifties who wore a matching maroon golf shirt and long cut coach's shorts with a silver whistle around his neck, to be a slave driver. The main point of his drills so far seemed to be to show the players that they were in no shape to play a "man's game" like football.

"I hope you guys enjoyed your summer, because it's over now," Coach Reynolds said, grinning slightly. "We're going to have to whip you into football shape in just three weeks. Anybody who's not ready for that knows where to turn in his practice gear."

Several players groaned again. It was either a reaction to the workload ahead or, more likely, Matt guessed, a reaction to Coach Reynolds' hard-nosed style. There had been only two practices, but already Matt found himself missing the more even approach of Coach Jim Stephens, for whom he had played baseball and basketball at South Side as a seventh-grader.

"We'll do some more conditioning later, when it cools down a little," the coach continued. "But right now we're going to work on positional play. I've got a coach stationed for quarterbacks, receivers, backs, defensive backs and linemen. So head on out to the station where you think you fit in best. We'll give you a shot at that position and then maybe move you around a bit before we decide where to put each of you."

Matt had been waiting to actually touch a football. Through the first practice the previous afternoon, the coaches hadn't even taken the balls out of the large duffel bags dutifully packed around by the team's half dozen student managers. The South Side prospects had simply worked on stretching, calisthenics and running for the entire ninety minutes before heading for home, sore and exhausted.

That sort of experience wasn't what Matt had in mind when he had decided, against his mother's protests, to go out for football. He had pictured himself as a wide receiver, streaking down the sidelines and gathering in long passes, scoring touchdowns and spiking the ball in the end zone as the fans in the stands cheered wildly...

"Hill! Are you going to join us?" Matt's thoughts were interrupted by Kevin Stone, an assistant coach and the offensive coordinator for the Stingers. Embarrassed to be caught day-dreaming, Matt hustled over to the fifteen or so kids who all wanted to be receivers.

It was a curious assortment of size, age and body type. At about five-foot-eight, Matt was in the middle of the group in terms of height and probably skinnier than most of the kids there. The tallest was Nate Brown, a ninth-grader who was already about six-foot-one and a blur in the open field. The shortest was five-foot-four Phil Wong, one of Matt's best friends who had also decided to go out for football as an eighth-grader.

"I know a lot of you kids have played football for a few years already," Coach Stone said, addressing the group. "But for the benefit of those who haven't, I'm going to go over a few basics of the receiver position."

Matt and Phil were among those the coach was referring to. Both had played organized basketball and baseball and even soccer, and both had thrown around the football plenty and played in pickup touch games in the neighborhood. But neither had strapped on football pads before, and their next real football tackle would also be their first. So far for these summer practices, they were wearing only shoulder pads, helmets and shorts, but even just having the pads sitting on his shoulders felt cumbersome and unnatural to Matt.

The coach explained how every receiver must run his "route" as if he was going to get the ball on every single play. If not, the defense eventually wouldn't bother covering him. Coach Stone showed the hopefuls how to get a quick start from a three-point stance off the snap of the ball. He then demonstrated how to catch the ball with the fingertips, absorbing the force of the pass before it hit the chest and securing the ball with two hands. Most of this just seemed like common sense to Matt. Somebody threw it and you ran fast and caught it. How hard could it be?

After watching the players catch passes from the coaches for fifteen minutes, Coach Stone blew his whistle. He motioned for Coach Reynolds to bring over the small group of quarterback prospects. There were only five boys in this group and they had all played football before. You had to be pretty confident in your abilities in order to go out for that position, Matt thought. The quarterback was the leader on offense and every play began with him. It wasn't a spot for somebody who wasn't absolutely sure of himself.

"Okay, guys," Coach Reynolds said. "We're going to have you run a few routes for the quarterbacks. Nothing fancy, just simple 'out' patterns. Let's do ten-yard routes, three-quarter speed. Quarterbacks, I want you to concentrate on footwork and form. Receivers, just try to run direct routes and make clean catches."

Matt felt his heart race. He had caught hundreds of footballs messing around with Phil and his other friends. But he had never touched the ball in a real practice before today. Looking at the drill lineups he realized that he would be paired with Ricky Jackson, a seventh-grader who was just entering South Side this fall. Jackson wasn't big, but he was muscular and he had a swagger that Matt thought was unusual for a rookie. Ricky Jackson had a sizable reputation. He had been the star in Pop Warner football during his elementary school days at Hillside and had won the regional Pass, Punt and Kick competition, getting to perform in front of thirty thousand fans during halftime of a college game at Eton last fall.

Matt also recognized Ricky as the younger brother of Grant Jackson. Matt and Grant had had plenty of conflict the previous winter. Matt was relieved that Grant was moving on to South Side High and wouldn't be around this year. But he wondered whether Jackson's little brother would be trouble too.

Matt and Jackson were paired in the fourth group of the drill. Following Coach Reynolds' instructions, Matt blasted off his three-point stance, ran ten yards downfield and cut sharply out to the right. Just as he made his move outside, Ricky Jackson delivered the ball on a perfect, tight spiral. Matt gathered the pass in full stride with his finger-tips, pulling it into his body, the way the coaches had shown them. It felt great to catch the ball like this with everybody watching.

"Nice job...Hill, is it?" Coach Reynolds barked. Matt nodded. So far, so good, he thought.

The passing drills continued for another fifteen minutes, with Coach Reynolds changing the routes of the receivers, from a ten-yard out, to a five-yard buttonhook, in which he directed the receivers to run straight ahead for a few steps, spin around and catch the ball in a play designed for short-yardage situations. Matt was paired with each of the quarterback prospects during these drills. He was most impressed with ninth-grader Kyle James, a lanky, six-foot left-hander who delivered the ball on a powerful line to his receivers. Matt knew James had shared the starter's job the previous season with ninth-grader Dave Tanner, who had since graduated. James was just about everybody's pick to be the South Side starter this year too.

Finally, Coach Reynolds called all the receivers into a huddle with the quarterback hopefuls. "Let's see how much speed you kids have," the coach said. "Now that you're warmed up, I want you to run a straight fly pattern at full speed. That means explode off the snap, and just keep running straight down the field. The QBs will hit you at about twenty yards. Everybody got it?"

The players nodded. Although they had been mixed with different quarterbacks throughout the drills, Matt did a mental count and noted he would be paired with Ricky Jackson once again for this drill. When it came their turn, he again shot off the line and headed downfield at full speed. About eighteen yards into his route, Matt slowed a tad as he turned his head backward, looking for the ball. Bad idea. Jackson had thrown the pass hard, trying to hit him on the dead run. The football was coming too high. Matt leapt as far as he could to grab it, but it wasn't even close. The ball landed beyond him, bouncing harmlessly down the turf.

Jackson removed his helmet and shook his head. Then Matt watched as he turned and glanced toward the chain-link fence that lined South Side's practice field.

Leaning over the fence was a large heavy-set man with graying hair, a reddish face and a maroon South Side cap, just like the ones the coaches wore. He was kicking at the grass and appeared to be muttering under his breath. Matt couldn't tell what he was saying, but it was pretty obvious he wasn't happy.

"Hill, you have to run the pattern right through," Coach Reynolds yelled. "You slowed down. That's an incompletion. Worse yet, it can cause an interception. Always finish your route."

Matt nodded. He knew he had made a mistake. The quarterbacks and receivers came together as the coach called for a final huddle at midfield. Matt glanced at Ricky Jackson, whose spiky black hair was soaked with sweat. "Sorry, man," he said to Jackson. "I should have kept running on that."

"Don't sweat it," Jackson replied, his dark eyes meeting Matt's across the huddle. "It's just a practice…No matter what my old man thinks."

Suddenly it all made sense to Matt. The man at the fence was Jackson's dad. And now Matt remembered him too. He had seen him in action a couple of times last basketball season. In fact, Coach Stephens and Mr. Jackson had had a loud run-in during practice after the coach had suspended Jackson's older son, Grant, for shop-lifting.

"Jackson, looks like your dad is already in mid-season form," joked Nate Brown. A couple of the other older players laughed. Jackson's face turned crimson. He said nothing and looked down. It was obvious the seventh-grader was embarrassed.

Matt knew Ricky was uncomfortable, but he couldn't relate to what he was feeling. His own father had left his mom when Matt was just three years old. He had often thought about how great it would be to have a dad come to all his games and practices, to take a keen interest in how he was doing in sports, maybe even to give him some pointers. But he had never even considered the possibility that having your father around could be embarrassing. Not until today.

chapter two

Before he even opened his eyes, Matt felt sore. His legs, arms, shoulders, even his feet, hurt. It was Thursday morning of the first week of full-contact football practice, and he was feeling it. Coach Reynolds had been right. This game wasn't for wimps.

Matt grimaced as he pushed the sheets off and swung his legs over the edge of the bed. Even that simple movement was painful. He had never felt this way before, not from baseball or basketball or any of the other sports he had played.

Three days of drills and scrimmages with full pads and equipment had meant three days of taking hits from the South Side defensive team, each of whom was trying to win a spot in the starting lineup. So as Matt had caught the ball on various patterns, he had been like fresh meat to a pack of tigers. He had taken his fair share of hits and then some over those three days.

Fortunately he began loosening up even as he went downstairs into the living room and opened the door to grab the *Post* off the front steps. It was the first thing he did every morning—find the newspaper and turn to the Sports section, lay it out on the kitchen counter with his breakfast and get himself up-to-date. It was a morning ritual that had started when he was in fifth grade. He couldn't get enough sports, either playing them or reading about them.

By the time his mother emerged from her bedroom, Matt had forgotten about his earlier aches.

"How's my boy, today?" She smiled, wrapping her arms around him and kissing him atop his wavy brown hair. Matt felt the soft fabric of her peach-colored housecoat on his ears and squeezed her left hand with his right. "I'm okay," he said.

"So, how's football practice going?" she asked. "At least you still look like you're in one piece."

Matt laughed. His mom had been dead-set against him going out for the South Side football team this year. It was a dangerous sport, she said. She had worried he would break an arm or a leg, or worse. But, as she had always done ever since he could remember, his mom had supported his decision and allowed him to try out.

"It's going pretty well," Matt replied. "You know, Mom, it's not much rougher than basketball. And you have all those pads on. It's fine. You'll see tomorrow."

"Tomorrow?" she asked. "What's happening then?"

Matt was surprised. He had been talking about the Maroon-and-White game all week at the dinner table with his mother. It was the South Side Stingers' annual pre-season intra-squad game, the last chance for prospects like Matt to prove they belonged on the team. It was only the most important moment in his football career.

"Mom, it's the…," he began.

"I'm teasing." She smiled. "I know, I know, it's your inter-team game, or whatever they call it."

Matt laughed. Just like Mom to screw up the name of something. "Intra-squad," he said slowly. "It's called that because we play against one another to show the coaches what we can do in a game situation. Are you coming?"

"I'm sorry," she said. "I can't make it. I've got an open house to do at the same time. I'd love to be there, though, to watch you score a run."

Matt groaned again. His mom actually had pretty decent knowledge about some sports—she had even played a little basketball in high school. But she knew absolutely nothing about football. Maybe that was why she wasn't keen on him going out for it. Her idea of the game was like something out of the International Wrestling Federation. She thought it was all hitting and punching and kicking and violence.

"We're only having a team meeting today," Matt said. "Coach says we have to rest our bodies after three days of contact."

Mom nodded. She was deep into a story on the front page of the *Post*. Matt could always tell when she was reading because she didn't return the conversation, at least not right away. When she was reading, she just nodded—kind of like he did when he was playing PlayStation and she was trying to talk to him.

Matt put his cereal bowl and spoon in the dishwasher. "I'll see you tonight," he said to his mom. She looked at him warmly. "Have a great day," she said.

Matt grabbed his backpack and headed out

the front door. It was only the first week of school, but already he felt he was well into the routine at South Side. Football practices had started two weeks prior to the first day of classes, so Matt had been walking this route for three weeks now. He picked up his pace as he headed down Anderson Crescent. Up ahead, under the big oak tree where Seventh Avenue dissected Anderson, he saw Phil and Jake, waiting for him as usual. The three had carried out the same routine since their days together at Glenview Elementary. Jake's dad called them the Three Amigos.

"At wide receiver, wearing number ten, in his second year at South Side Middle School, Maaattttt Hiiiilllll," Jake bellowed in an over-the-top announcer's voice. "How's the football star this morning?"

"Give it a rest, man." Matt grinned. "I didn't feel too much like a star getting out of bed today."

"Me neither," interjected Phil. "I've never been so sore in my life."

"You two should try riding one of my uncle's horses sometime." Jake laughed. "You want to wake up sore…"

Matt couldn't help thinking that Jake Piancato should be going out for football this year too.

Matt's closest friend since preschool days was already about five-foot-ten and had the kind of bouncy athleticism that would make him a natural at just about any position on the field. Jake was a big football fan too, watching National Football League games on Sundays and often wearing a number 4 Green Bay Packers jersey with the name *Favre* on the back.

But Jake simply couldn't commit the time to football in the fall. His family ran Long Lake Lodge, about a ten-minute drive out of town. And although autumn was football season, it was also fishing season. The lodge was booked solid during September and October, and the Piancatos couldn't drive Jake back and forth for practice every day during this time of the year. They also needed him to help out around the lodge after school and on weekends during this busy season.

That didn't prevent Jake from taking a keen interest in the South Side Stingers football team, however. "How's practice going, Matty?" he asked. "Are you going to start at receiver?"

Matt shook his head. "It's not like touch football, Jake," he said. "You only get a play called for you every so often and guys are drilling you pretty good when you catch one. I've dropped a few this week."

"Yeah," Phil added wearily. "The game's a lot different with pads on."

But Phil didn't have to worry about dropping anything that afternoon, because Coach Reynolds was taking it easy on his players after nearly three weeks of constant practice. As the fifty boys gathered on the sidelines, the coach blew his silver whistle.

"Okay, people, come on in," he said, motioning the players to gather around a large blackboard on wheels he had rolled out to the sidelines. The front of the board was facing away from the team.

"We're not going to practice today," Coach Reynolds said. "I just want to go over a few things with you before the Maroon-and-White game tomorrow."

The players watched attentively as the coach began to turn the board around. It was divided into two halves by a single yellow chalk line. Half of their names were on one side, listed under their positions. Half of their names were on the other. Matt's name was on the left side, under the White team. Phil's was on the right, with the Maroon squad.

"These are your teams for the intra-squad," the coach said. "We'll be running basic offense and defense, just the things you've worked on in practice, so nobody should have problems remembering plays.

"But you should be aware of this," the coach continued. "We will have to make a few cuts this year. There are about twenty of you who won't make the team. I'm sorry about that, but we don't have the coaches or the equipment to run a junior varsity. I will be announcing the roster on Monday. Please remember, if you don't make it, there are other ways you can contribute to South Side football."

The coach didn't keep them long. In fact, it had hardly been worth getting changed. Matt and Phil were out of the locker room quickly and walking home before five o'clock.

"I hope we both make it," Phil said as they neared the end of the first block.

"Don't worry, Philly, how could they cut two future NFL stars like us?" Matt said, pulling Phil's maroon South Side baseball cap down over his eyes.

"It's not you I'm worried about," Phil said, his broad face creasing with concern. "I'm just not sure there's room on this team for a small, slow Chinese kid."

Matt laughed. Phil was always poking fun at himself. But he was a terrific athlete. Although short, he was much stronger than he looked and he had a rifle for an arm. Phil was a terrific catcher and a dependable hitter in baseball, his best sport. And he had developed into a major three-point threat in basketball. He had been struggling to find the right position in football, though. He didn't have the type of speed needed to consistently get open and he was smaller than all the defensive backs on the South Side roster.

"I'm sure you'll do just fine," Matt said reassuringly. They were already at the corner of Anderson and Seventh, the place where they parted ways each day. Phil would continue on to Wong's Grocery, the corner store run by his grandmother, and Matt would head home. "Catch you tomorrow," Matt said.

Matt was deep in thought the rest of the way home. He had tried to sound confident in front of Phil, but he knew neither of them was guaranteed a spot on the team. Both were new to the sport and both had experienced their share of ups and downs during practice. The Maroon-and-White game was going to be a big test for both of them.

chapter three

It was strange. This wasn't even a real game, but Matt felt his stomach fluttering worse than it had ever done before any big game in any other sport he had played. Even his legs felt weak and shaky as he ran through the calisthenics White team captain Kyle James was leading on their half of the South Side field.

Matt had been placed on the same team as a pair of star ninth-graders—James, the team's likely starter at quarterback, and Nate Brown, the tall receiver with the blazing speed. Matt wasn't starting. In fact he was listed under Brown on the depth chart that assistant coach Kevin Stone had drawn up. Coach Stone was controlling the Whites for this scrimmage while Coach Reynolds had the Maroon team. There were fifty boys suited up this afternoon, with many of them fighting for one of the forty spots on the final South Side roster.

It might not be a real game, but Coach Reynolds had hired real officials for it, and already, there were a couple of hundred people in the bleachers that lined one side of the field. Of all the sports at South Side, football drew the most community interest. Even people who had no formal ties to the school seemed to be interested in how the Stingers were doing on the field. That was one of the reasons Matt had wanted so badly to go out for football this year. He wanted to be part of the biggest thing in school sports, even if he didn't have a single down of experience.

The whistle sounded and both Kyle James and Nate Brown jogged to midfield to talk to the officials, along with the captains of the Maroon squad. It was impossible to tell the two Maroon captains apart. They were the Evans twins, Reggie and Ron. The two ninth-graders had long, fiery red hair and freckles and both played the linebacker position. Their tough run-and-pass coverage and open-field hits were major reasons why the South Side defense figured to be one of the best in the league this year.

The Maroon side won the coin toss, and the Evans boys elected to receive the kick. Nate lined up the football on the tee near midfield, and as the whistle again sounded, the game was on. Brown booted the ball deep into the Maroon zone, about twenty yards short of the goal line. Phil, who was starting on special teams, drew a bead on the ball, preparing to catch it. But as he stretched out his arms to grab the football, he stumbled slightly, throwing off his timing. The ball bounced off his arms and right into the hands of an oncoming White player who was gang-tackled at the twenty-yard line. On the first play of the game, Phil had made a huge mistake.

Knowing it would be a tough error to make up for, Matt watched his friend shuffle off the field, head down. Meanwhile, the play continued with White quarterback Kyle James lining up behind hulking center Steve Donnelly, an eighth-grader who was so wide that Matt literally had to walk around him in the corridor at school. Matt had often thought it must be difficult to be so huge, but size was a big advantage playing on the line in football. Donnelly, wearing number 75, provided enough protection all on his own to give James plenty of time to find an open receiver.

Sure enough, the quarterback located an open man right off the first snap. Brown ran a ten-yard out pattern to the right side, and James delivered the ball perfectly. Brown torched the defensive back trying to cover him and scampered the ten remaining yards into the end zone. One play was all it took and the White team had scored a touchdown.

By halftime, the Whites had scored two more times and led 21–7. The only time the Maroon team had managed to penetrate the White side of the field was on a long touchdown pass from quarterback Ricky Jackson to Reggie Evans, one of the twins, who also sometimes doubled as a slot back.

Until then, Matt had only been in the game for one play—the kickoff following his team's third touchdown. And on that sequence he hadn't managed to get near the Maroon ball carrier. The sweat he had worked up during pre game warm ups had dried as he sat in the locker room, waiting for the halftime talk from Coach Stone.

"Hill!" the coach yelled. Matt looked up. "You're going in for Brown on offense to start the third quarter."

Matt was happy for the chance to play, but nervous about filling in for Brown, who had scored two of the team's three touchdowns in the first half. Matt nodded to the coach. He was so focused on the fact he was getting a chance to play that he had trouble concentrating on the halftime instructions.

As the players trotted back onto the field, Matt knew that this was his time to make an impression. If he wanted to play football at South Side, he would have to get something done in this half. Otherwise, why would the coaches keep an eighth-grader, when they could put a seventh-grader in the lineup and have him around for an extra year? It wasn't like Matt was huge or had outstanding speed. He was a good athlete but rather unremarkable, he thought, when it came to his football skills. Worst of all, he had no experience at the game. Many of the other kids out here had been playing community football since their grade-school days.

The White team would be receiving the ball to start the second half, and Matt took Brown's spot on the return team too. He was one of two players lined up deep to receive the kickoff, the other being beefy fullback Pete Cowan, a short ninth-grader with huge shoulders and no neck.

The whistle sounded and Ricky Jackson swung his foot through the football, booting it on a high arc toward the goal line. It was to Cowan's side of the field, so Matt ran ahead of his team-mate, looking to throw a block for him. Cowan caught the football on the dead run and headed left, straight toward Matt. As Matt turned, he saw Phil streaking downfield. Phil launched himself at Cowan, but Matt stepped in front, using his shoulder to block his path. The block sprung Pete free. He headed upfield for twenty yards before he was finally brought down.

"Great run, Pete!" Coach Stone shouted from the sidelines. "And nice block, Hill. Way to spring him."

Matt's ears were burning. The praise was nice, but he also felt badly for Phil, who had missed the tackle, another strike against him in this intra-squad game.

The White team went into a huddle, a few yards behind the football, which was positioned at their own thirty-five-yard line. Kyle James called the first play, a run up the middle for Cowan. All of the receivers had routes to run on this play too. Matt knew his was a down-and-out, ten yards going right.

Matt remembered Coach Reynolds' words at that first practice three weeks earlier. *Run every route like you're getting the ball.* He went into his three-point stance on the right side, waited for the snap count, and then he exploded off the line. Reggie Evans picked him up in the backfield and shadowed him to the right side. Meanwhile, the ball had been handed off to Cowan, who burst through the area just vacated by Matt for a ten-yard run. Although he hadn't caught the ball himself, Matt suddenly realized how important it was to convince his defender that he was expecting the pass. Had Reggie Evans suspected that Matt wasn't looking for the football, he could have cheated and helped stop Cowan much sooner.

The White team continued to move the ball steadily downfield. They were clearly superior to the Maroon defense, even though Coach Reynolds had tried to make the teams relatively even. With a first down on the Maroon thirty-yard line, the Whites went into their huddle. Kyle James turned to face Matt. "Hill, this is yours. Twenty-yard fly. Straight up the middle. You ready?"

Matt nodded. He didn't feel ready, though. His legs were weak as he lined up. This was the first pass play ever called for him. He heard the snap count and again fired off the line, heading straight up the field just as the play required.

But Reggie Evans was right on his tail, as if he smelled the call by James. Matt turned to look for the ball. There it was, on a perfect line, heading for him. He reached up, it was in his fingers. And then it wasn't. Matt watched in disgust as the ball slipped from his grasp and bounced to the turf. He wasn't sure whether it was hearing Evans behind him or just the fact his hands were shaking. Whatever it was, he had dropped the ball. What a loser!

Matt heard the crowd in the bleachers groan. He trotted back to the huddle and looked sheepishly at Kyle James. "Hill, same thing," the senior quarterback said, matter-of-factly. "On two." Matt was stunned. After he had dropped a great pass, James was going right back to him? Why?

He didn't have time to argue. Once again, Matt lined up and burst off the snap. This time, however, Reggie Evans wasn't following him nearly as closely. It was clear that the linebacker didn't think the ball was going to Matt for a second straight play. He was wrong. Matt looked back as he reached the twenty-yard mark and saw the ball, again heading toward him in a tight spiral. He didn't have to jump or even stretch much. All he had to do was catch the ball. This time he did just that, grabbing the football with his fingertips and pulling it into his body. He didn't break stride, and Evans was left behind as Matt headed into the end zone untouched. The fans in the bleachers cheered. This is just how he had imagined it!

Matt was elated. In his first Maroon-and-White game, he had scored a touchdown. But the feeling was short-lived as he reached the sideline. "Nice catch," Coach Stone said. "Have a seat. Vickers is in for you next series."

That was it for Matt in this game. Despite his catch, this was an intra-squad contest and it was designed so that the coaches could get a good look at all the players. Matt had to hope that the one catch would be enough to land him a spot on the South Side team.

As the half continued, Matt's replacement, Keith Vickers, also played well in the wide receiver spot. He made a couple of tough catches, one a diving reception off a poorly thrown ball. Vickers was small, but he was quicker than Matt and he was only in the seventh grade. Matt had already figured out that to make the South Side team, he would probably have to beat Vickers out for the spot. He didn't know if he'd done that in this game or not.

Meanwhile, Phil was continuing to struggle on the Maroon side. He caught only one of four balls thrown his way, and although he hustled on every special-teams' play and was in on a couple of tackles, Matt knew his friend would be on the bubble to make the Stingers too.

After the final whistle had blown on a 42–21 win for the Whites, Coach Reynolds called both squads to midfield. It was seven o'clock and already beginning to get dark with a slight chill creeping into the air. The players each took one knee in a circle around the head coach.

"Nice job today, kids," Coach Reynolds said, his voice softer than Matt remembered from try-outs. "You guys made some pretty good football plays today. I think we're going to have another successful season at South Side.

"I know practice has been tough on you for the last three weeks. Now comes the tough part for me and the other coaches. We'll be doing cuts this weekend. Check the gym bulletin board for the final roster on Monday morning. And remember, if your name's not up there, it doesn't mean you can't be part of the program in some way.

"Now have a good weekend. We'll start preparing Monday afternoon for our first real game."

Matt was tired. It had been a long, pressure-filled afternoon. Nevertheless, he knew he'd have trouble sleeping this weekend. There was some big news coming Monday and right now he wasn't sure whether it was going to be good or bad.

chapter four

Matt hurried home, eager to tell his mom about the game. He was walking alone because Phil's parents had picked him up from school to visit his cousins downtown. As he waved good-bye, Matt could tell that Phil was worried about his chances of making the team.

All in all, Matt felt pretty good about how he himself had performed. Sure, he had messed up on a couple of plays, particularly on the first deep route that Kyle James had called for him. But the fact that James had called his number again, the very next play no less, had given Matt a boost of confidence. Why would he do that unless he thought Matt was capable of catching the football?

A block from home, Matt noticed an unfamiliar vehicle in the driveway, parked behind his mom's shiny green Toyota Camry. It was a sleek black Ford SUV, with oversized tires. It must belong to one of Mom's real estate clients, Matt thought. She had been showing a house today. Maybe they were already writing up a deal. Matt certainly hoped that was the case. It had been a slow summer for Mom selling houses, and she was stressing about work more than usual.

It was still warm enough that only the screen door was closed on the house, so Matt slipped inside without his mom hearing. He could hear voices coming from the living room. Turning the corner from the front hallway, he saw his mom sitting on the sofa, across from a tall angular man with brown wavy hair. He was dressed in a dark sports coat and tan pants. Matt immediately sensed the tension in the room. This was no real estate deal.

"Matt, will you come with me for a minute, please," his mom said, without even first saying hello or introducing him to the visitor. This was strange. Matt knew something was up, but what? Was he in trouble for something he didn't know about? Had somebody in the family died?

Was his mom sick? All sorts of thoughts were racing through his head.

Mom grabbed his hand and led him through the sliding door into the kitchen. She closed the door, and then she turned toward him. "This is really hard…," she began tentatively.

What was hard? Matt was now starting to panic. His stomach was flopping about even worse than it had been before today's intra-squad game. What was going on here, anyway?

"I'm just going to say it," Mom finally blurted out. "I'm not sure if you recognize him, Matt. I didn't want it to be like this for you. He just showed up here this afternoon. ...The man in the living room is Tom Jensen. He's your father, Matt."

Matt felt himself getting light-headed. He sat down on the stool by the kitchen eating bar and tried to comprehend what he had just heard. His father? It had been so long since his father had been in his life that Matt had nearly forgotten he had one, somewhere out there. The visitor had seemed familiar, but the only pictures Matt had ever seen of his dad were by now at least ten years old. It hadn't clicked who this man was until he heard the words from his mother's mouth. Matt didn't know how to react. This was the weirdest feeling he had ever experienced.

"It's up to you, Matt," Mom continued gently. "If you don't want to talk to him right now, I'm sure he'll understand. I certainly understand. I know it's a shock…"

"What's he doing here, Mom?" Matt said, in a cross between a yell and a whisper. "I mean, why now?"

Matt's dad had been out of their lives for ten years, ever since his parents split up when he was just three. It had always seemed strange and it had always hurt that the man had never kept in contact. Matt had other friends whose parents were divorced, and most of their dads had stayed active in their lives. He had just always assumed his own dad didn't care enough to do that. He began to feel angry at the man sitting in the next room.

"I don't know," Matt stammered. "I don't know what to do."

"You know what?" his mom said. "I'm just going to tell him to go. This isn't fair to you. You haven't had a chance to prepare. I'm sorry, Matt."

His head was whirling. Part of him wanted to go tell the man in the next room to get out of their house, to go away and never come back. Part of him was frightened about facing up to such a big moment in his life. Another part of him was curious. His dad? He had always wondered what his dad was like.

"Wait, Mom," Matt said softly. "I'll meet him."

She stretched out her arms and hugged her son, her small hands wrapping around the back of his neck. "Come on, then."

His mother slowly slid the pocket door open. The visitor was standing by the front window. He turned as he heard the kitchen door slide open.

Matt was caught completely off guard. It was a bizarre feeling, like looking into a mirror. The man was tall, about six-foot-four, and thin—not rakishly thin, but athletically slim. He had brown eyes and wavy brown hair. The only thing radically different between he and Matt, besides age, was that his nose was larger and much more pointed. Matt had the round small nose of his mother.

"Hello, Matt," the man said, clearly nervous himself. "It's been a long time."

A long time? Matt felt as though he had never ever met this man. They might look alike but they had nothing in common. Matt couldn't remember having done a single thing with his father. The anger and frustration built up over ten years was welling up inside him again.

The man stretched out a large right hand with long slender fingers. Matt responded, shaking his father's hand. The ritual felt stilted, unnatural.

"Your mom tells me that you're quite an athlete," the man said. "I loved sports myself when I was a kid."

Matt nodded. He didn't know what to say. His voice seemed lost in the moment. He wanted to talk to his dad, to ask him questions, especially about why he had never bothered to show up or contact him until now. But he couldn't get anything out.

"I've actually been to a couple of your football practices," the visitor said. "You've got good hands."

"You were at my practices?" Matt asked incredulously. "Why?"

"I just wanted to see you, Matt," he said. "I thought it would be too much of a shock to just introduce myself to you, especially at a football practice. This afternoon, I was just coming here to talk to your mother, to figure out what would be the best way to meet you. I didn't realize you'd be coming home so soon. We both thought you would still be practicing. I'm sorry it happened like this.

"I've been out of the country for almost ten years, working in Saudi Arabia as an air-craft mechanic," he continued, now rushing his words. "But I'm back now and I guess it's about time we met."

Matt was confused. How should he feel about this? Happy to have a dad, finally? Or angry that his dad didn't care enough to even send a birthday card for the last ten years? There wasn't an easy answer here. He stared at his father. Nobody said a word. The silence was uncomfortable.

"Listen," his father finally said. "I've got to go now. I didn't expect you to be home. But I'm glad you were here. It's great to see you, son."

Son? The word felt false and awkward to Matt's ears.

"Can I take you out for lunch tomorrow?" the man asked, hopefully. "I could pick you up and we could go somewhere, catch up a little."

Matt wasn't sure. He looked at his mother, who had been silent. Then he looked back at the visitor.

"I usually play basketball on Saturday mornings," he said slowly. " But I guess I could, after that."

"How about one o'clock, then?" the man said. "I'll pick you up here."

Matt glanced at his mother again. She simply shrugged her shoulders and arched her eyebrows. "It's completely up to you, Matt," she said.

"I guess so," he said, shaking his father's hand again.

"Great! I'll see you tomorrow."

With that, the man turned, said a quick goodbye to Matt's mom, rounded the corner into the hallway, opened the screen door and walked down the front sidewalk. Matt watched out the living room window as the lanky figure eased into the front seat of the dark suv and began to back up out of the driveway. He noticed Matt looking and waved. Matt slowly brought up his hand to return the gesture.

He turned to his mom, shaking his head. "That was too weird," Matt declared.

Mom was sitting on the couch, a serious look on her face and her eyes were welling up. Matt hated to see her cry. He sat down beside her and put his arm on her shoulder. She sobbed softly, and as he sat there, Matt felt powerless to help.

They didn't say anything for the longest time. Matt was lost in thought too. He now had two parents, like most of the kids he knew. But at this moment, he couldn't find the words to talk with either of them.

chapter five

After a quiet dinner, Matt helped load the dish-washer.

"I'm tired, Matt," his mother said. "I've got to take some clients out early tomorrow. I think I'd better go to bed."

"Okay, Mom," he said.

She turned and hugged him. The hug felt good, secure in a way, on a night when his world had been turned upside down.

"I just want you to know that you have to make your own choices regarding your father," she said. "You need to know that I'm okay with it if you have a relationship with him. I mean, if you want, that is…"

Matt kissed his mom goodnight and she headed toward her bedroom. He was in no mood to sleep, though. So much was running through his mind. He was having lunch with his father the next day. What was he supposed to say? And just what could the man possibly say that would make up for him being gone for all those years?

Matt felt like he needed to talk to his brother about this. So he grabbed the cordless phone and headed up to his bedroom. He was pretty sure Mark would be home now, no matter whether he had worked overtime today or not. Eight years older, Mark had a good-paying job on the oil rigs near Eton, a few hours away by car. Mark had been eleven when their father left home, not much younger than Matt was now. He wondered how his brother would react to the news that their father was coming back into their lives.

Mark picked up on the third ring. "Hey, little bro," he said. "What's up?"

Matt quickly launched into the afternoon's events, how the presence of his father had shocked him and how Mom had seemed quiet and sad during the entire visit. He told Mark about his lunch date the next day.

"Well, that's up to you, I guess," Mark said. His voice suddenly sounded a little bit cooler to Matt.

"I'm not having anything to do with that guy," his brother continued. "He called me earlier this week and left a message. I haven't called him back. As far as I'm concerned, he doesn't exist. ...He can't just come back ten years later and pretend nothing happened. It doesn't work that way."

Matt was surprised by the sudden hostility in his brother's voice. It didn't sound like Mark at all. Normally, he was so easygoing and levelheaded. Right now, he sounded angry and hurt. Matt knew the emotions weren't directed at him but they made him feel uncomfortable nonetheless.

"But what should *I* do?" Matt asked. "I already said I'd have lunch with him…"

"Like I said, that's up to you," Mark said; then he suddenly shifted gears. "How's Mom, anyway?"

"She's in bed already," Matt replied. "I don't know. She seemed kind of bummed, I guess."

There was a long pause, and then Mark continued. "Matt, you were pretty young when Dad left. Too young to understand it all, obviously. But when he went, he left Mom pretty broken up. It took her a long time to recover. That's never going to be okay with me. Whenever I do talk to him, that's what I'm going to tell him."

Matt tried to imagine having a father and then losing him around the same age he was right now. It obviously would have been a difficult situation for Mark. Which was worse, having a dad for a few years or not having one at all?

"I've got to go, kid," Mark said. "I've got another call coming in. But you take it easy, okay? Do what you think is right. Send me an e-mail tomorrow and let me know how it goes."

Matt had difficulty getting to sleep. He rolled around in his bed, trying to get comfortable. But all he could think of was lunch tomorrow and what he was going to say to his dad.

He awoke early the next morning to sunshine streaming through his bedroom window. He had forgotten to close the heavy drapes on his east-facing room. Matt looked at the clock. It was only 8:00 AM and it was Saturday. He contemplated going back to bed, but decided that would be futile. Instead, he headed downstairs and directly to the front door, which he opened, and scooped up the *Post* off the front step.

Matt turned immediately to the Sports section, pulled down a cereal bowl from the cupboard and poured himself some Cheerios. He was just shoving the first spoonful into his mouth when he saw the picture on the second page of the Sports section. It was Phil! But he wasn't going to like the shot. It showed the ball ricocheting off his hands, one of several passes that he had dropped during the Maroon-and-White game the previous day. You could see the anxious look on Phil's face as the ball slipped away. In terms of action, it was a great picture, but it wasn't very flattering to his friend.

Matt hadn't thought about football since yesterday evening. All he could think about now was the lunch today with his dad. It consumed him all morning, as he played three-on-three basketball at Anderson Park with Phil, Jake, Amar Sunir and a couple of other friends.

"What's up, Mattster?" Jake said as they took a water break. "You've hardly made a shot all morning. Worried about making the football team, or what?"

"I guess so," Matt replied. He wasn't ready yet to tell his friends about his dad. It was such weird news, he didn't even know how to bring it up. He also didn't know how he felt about it yet.

The game broke up about eleven thirty, and Matt headed home, had a long shower and got ready to meet his father. It was weird, but he fretted over what clothes to wear and took extra time to comb his hair. Why was he so concerned about what he looked like? He couldn't figure it out. But at the same time it seemed important.

Just before one o'clock, the black Ford SUV rolled into the driveway. Matt's dad eased out of the front seat and walked to the front door. His mom was already out doing an open house, so Matt had been waiting near the door for his father. Might as well get this over with, he thought. He met the visitor outside.

"Hey, Matt," his father said cheerily. "Are you hungry?"

Matt nodded. He wasn't really. He was too nervous to even think of eating. He climbed into the passenger seat of the SUV and did up his seatbelt. His father slid into the driver's seat and turned to him.

"Know anywhere we can get a good pizza?" his dad asked.

"We always go to Classico's," Matt replied. "It's not far from here."

They exchanged small talk about the SUV, the weather, football and pizza as they drove. At the restaurant, a waitress led them to a secluded table near the back.

Shortly after they had ordered, Matt's dad laid his palms down on the table and cleared his throat.

"I know you must have some questions," he said, suddenly looking nervous. "But maybe first I'll tell you where I've been for the last ten years…"

Strangely, Matt giggled. Just a nervous reaction. "Sure," he said. "Okay."

His father cleared his throat again, raised his eyebrows and sighed.

"Well, Matt, your mother and I had been married for about ten years. We got married young. We had Mark very young. I thought getting married was the right thing to do, so did your mother. But we weren't ready. I mean, I guess more honestly, I wasn't ready.

"By the time you came along, we were fighting a lot. We didn't seem to like each other much anymore. I was working as an aircraft mechanic and was out of town a lot. Your mother was lonely."

Where was he going with all this? Matt wondered. This was his excuse for not being around for ten years?

"I made a mistake, Matt," his father continued. "I got involved with another woman, somebody

I met when I was away on a job. It was a stupid thing to do. I told your mother about it. She asked me to leave, and I don't blame her. It was my fault."

Matt's head was reeling. It was making more sense now. No wonder his mother didn't talk much about his dad. Matt felt himself again growing angry at the man sitting across the booth.

"Your mother asked me to move out and I did," his father said. "Right about the same time, I got a job offer to work in Saudi Arabia. The money was good, and it was a chance to get away. I took it. And that's where I've been until now."

A chance to get away? From what? From his own kids? Matt couldn't believe what he was hearing.

"But why didn't you at least keep in touch?" he said. "I thought you didn't care about us. It still seems like that."

His father looked hurt. His voice cracked.

"That was never true, Matt," he said. "I've thought about you and Mark every day since I left. I've missed you guys so much. ...But your mother was so angry with me. At that time, it just seemed like the best thing to do was to leave her alone. I sent money regularly, but she never cashed the checks. They all came back to me in the mail."

Matt sat silently, stone-faced. He didn't know how to respond.

"I know now that cutting off contact was the wrong thing to do," his father continued. "I've missed out on so much by doing that, and you kids have too. I'm sorry, Matt. If I could do it over again, I would."

"So, why are you back now?" Matt asked. "Why change now, after all this time?"

The man sighed again. "Maybe I've grown up," he said. "I know it sounds strange, but over the last few months, I decided it was time to come home, try to salvage something with my kids. I can understand your mother has concerns about it, but I want to get to know you and your brother, Matt, to be part of your lives again, if you'll let me."

At that moment, the waitress arrived at the booth with their extra-large, double-cheese, double-pepperoni and onions pizza, just like Matt ordered every time he came to Classico's. The two took advantage of the food to stop the awkward conversation and just eat.

Matt wasn't that hungry. But munching down

pizza was easier than talking. Besides the pep-
peroni, he was trying to digest everything he had
just heard. At least now he knew where his dad
had been all these years and why he hadn't bothered to contact the family, even if it still seemed
like a bit of a lame excuse. And he certainly
understood why his mother had been reluctant
to talk about his dad.

They finished the pizza. "So what do you say,
Matt?" his father asked, nursing a cup of coffee.

"About what?"

"About you and me. Can we have a relationship? I'd like that…"

"I guess so," Matt replied, without thinking.

"Great!" his dad said. "Great!"

They drove back down Anderson toward
Matt's house. His father pulled into the driveway
and turned off the ignition. "I'll call your mother
and see if it's okay if I come to your next football
game," he said.

"I haven't even made the team yet," Matt
replied. "Final cuts are Monday. Better wait till
then at least."

Matt's dad smiled and winked. "No need to
wait. I'm sure you'll be on the team. I saw the
intra-squad game. We'll see you next week,
okay?"

Matt nodded. He jumped out of the SUV, closed the door and waved to his father. Waved to his father? The thought of it was bizarre.

He was glad Mom wasn't home as he unlocked the front door. His head was churning, full of conflicting ideas about his father's return to their lives. Part of him felt guilty about even being out to lunch with his dad. His mother obviously had mixed feelings at best about the man's return, and Mark had made it perfectly clear that he wasn't about to resume a relationship with their father. But another part of Matt felt excited about having a father who took interest in him, his school and his sports. As he headed into the house, he wondered why life had to be so complicated.

chapter six

The double doors to the South Side gym were closed when Matt, Phil and Jake arrived early Monday morning. It was still twenty minutes before advisory began, but Matt and Phil had wanted to get to the gym early, knowing that Coach Reynolds was posting the football roster on the bulletin board. Jake was simply tagging along to see who made it and who didn't.

They joined the crowd already standing in front of the bulletin board, surveying the list of names. The coach had drawn up a depth chart, with players listed by position, instead of merely a straight roster. Once they got close enough, Matt scanned the offensive side of the chart. If he was going to be on the team, it would be as an offensive player since he hadn't run any drills with the defense.

His eyes immediately went to the receiver category, which was topped by Nate Brown. Typed right below Brown's name was *Hill, Matthew.* He had made it. He was on the Stingers football team. Matt hadn't thought a lot about the cuts over the weekend. His mind had been preoccupied by his father's sudden reappearance. But this was both huge news and a major relief.

Matt continued looking down the depth chart. But just as he had feared, Phil's name wasn't there. He was pretty sure, judging by Phil's mood this morning on the way to school, that his buddy had already resigned himself to the fact he wasn't going to make the team. Phil hadn't done anything outstanding in practice, and he had made several mistakes in the Maroon-and-White game. Given his size and his lack of football experience, it had been a long shot for Phil Wong to make the team from the beginning.

"Hey, Matt, nice going," Phil said, smiling. "I knew you would make it."

"Sorry, Philly," Matt replied. "I was hoping to see your name up there too."

"That's okay," Phil replied. "I'll just gear up early for basketball season, I guess. Anyway, Grandma needs help around the store so…"

Matt thought that Phil was just making excuses. He knew his friend must be disappointed. But there wasn't much he could do about it.

Matt turned his attention back to the team roster. The quarterback spot was no surprise. Kyle James was listed as the starter, with Ricky Jackson second and Keith Vickers third. Now there was an interesting selection, Matt thought. Vickers was the seventh-grader who had been trying out for receiver, the kid whom Matt felt he had to beat out for a spot on the team. But Vickers could also throw the ball and was pretty quick. It was a smart move for Coach to keep him on the roster, playing receiver and getting some reps in at quarterback too.

One figure eyeing the depth chart stood out. Matt recognized Mr. Jackson, Ricky's father. He didn't look happy. Shaking his head, Mr. Jackson strode toward the coaches' office. Just then, the warning bell rang for the daily twenty-minute advisory period. Matt had to hurry if he was going to make it across campus in time.

For the second straight year, Matt had drawn Ms. Dawson as his advisory teacher. He considered himself lucky. She was a tall, dark-haired woman with hazel eyes and a warm, welcoming way about her that made everyone feel comfortable. Matt had enjoyed these advisory periods last year.

Ms. Dawson had a different theme almost every day. Sometimes it was a piece of news the class would discuss, sometimes she would stick a CD into the mini stereo on her desk and then break down what the lyrics meant with the students. Today she simply wrote one word on the blackboard: *Forgiveness*.

"This is a confusing time in your lives," she told the students. "There are all kinds of things coming your way—drugs, sex and peer pressure to do all kinds of stuff.

"But what I wanted to talk about today is the concept of forgiveness. Nobody gets through middle school without making some kind of mistake. It's a time in your life when you're finding out who you are. You are bound to screw up once in awhile, right?"

Heads nodded all around the room.

"So I guess forgiveness is important in a couple of ways," Ms. Dawson continued. "First, we must be able to find it in ourselves to forgive other people who do things they shouldn't. We shouldn't give up on our friends if they make a mistake, right? We wouldn't want them to give up on us.

"And second, we need to learn how to forgive ourselves. That's important too. You need to know that it's okay to make mistakes and that you'll learn from them. You need to know that you can carry around the knowledge of what you've learned from making those mistakes. But don't carry around the guilt. Forgive yourself. You deserve it."

Matt was confused. And judging by the looks on the faces of his fellow students, he wasn't the only one. This hadn't been one of Ms. Dawson's better sessions. When the bell rang, he rushed out of the classroom. He couldn't wait to get through the school day and on to practice. The Stingers would be getting their uniforms today. Sweet.

At the end of the day Matt stuffed the books he didn't need into his locker and headed to the gym. A long table with South Side jerseys, helmets and football pants was set up in the middle of the basketball floor, with Charlie Dougan heading up a football assembly line.

A smallish ninth-grader with short blond hair, Dougan had been the manager of the baseball team last spring and had helped Matt a great deal with his hitting. Matt saw that the large brace Charlie had worn on his left leg for the past year was gone, although he still seemed to be limping a little.

The players lined up to receive their gear. Matt was excited. Three weeks of practice had paid off. He was on the team, a second-stringer maybe, but on the team just the same. As he drew closer to the table, Matt noticed Phil Wong standing beside Charlie Dougan, talking to the manager. Phil nodded his head, went to the equipment room, grabbed a box and brought it to Charlie.

"Hey, Phil," Matt said as he got closer to the table. "What's going on?"

"I'm going to be a manager." Phil smiled. "I talked to Coach about it this morning. There's more than one way to be part of this football team."

Matt grinned. He was happy to see Phil being so positive after the disappointment of not making the roster. Matt didn't think he would have been so gracious in the same situation.

After collecting their gear, the team gathered around Coach Reynolds. It was raining hard outside, so there would be no practice today.

"Listen up, people," the coach said. "First of all, congratulations on making the Stingers. That's a real accomplishment and due to three weeks or more of hard work.

"But let's remember, our real work is just beginning. We play North Vale on Friday night. We have only three days of practice to get ready. I'm going to need all your concentration for those three days or we're going to go out there and fall on our faces. And boys, I don't like falling on my face."

The players chuckled.

"So take these uniforms home, show them off to your parents and friends and girlfriends. But then store them away until North Vale. Come back tomorrow in your ratty old practice gear and be ready to sweat."

chapter seven

Matt could hardly wait to get home to tell his mom that he had made the football team. She must have heard him coming up the steps because she met him at the door.

"So?" she said, drawing out the word. "What happened?"

"I'm on the team," Matt said triumphantly. "We got our uniforms today and we've got a game against North Vale on Friday after school. Can you make it?"

"I'll be there, Matt," she replied. "I wouldn't miss it. Just please, please promise me you'll try not to get hurt. I don't think I could handle seeing that."

Matt spent most of dinner going over the Stingers' schedule with his mom. Although she clearly didn't know much about football, she listened attentively to him explain how the team's season would unfold. Unlike basketball, South Side played each other team in the district middle school league only once. The league had only six teams, since three area schools did not field football squads. Coach Reynolds had said that it cost $20,000 a season just to put a team on the field and that they should consider themselves lucky because the South Side booster club raised those funds every year.

"I'm proud of you for making the team, Matt," his mom said. "But I need to tell you, your father called when you were at practice today. He wants to know if it's okay if he comes to your game Friday too."

For most of the day, Matt had managed to forget about his dad. Making the football team, getting his uniform and all the excitement that went along with that had for the time being taken his mind off the big news in his personal life.

"I'm okay with it, if you are," Matt said, eyeing his mother carefully. "I mean, I'd understand if you weren't."

Mom put her fork down and looked at Matt. "This isn't about me," she said seriously. "This is about you. We aren't going to be sitting together or anything, so if your father decides to come to the game, it won't affect me one way or another. It should be whatever you're comfortable with, Matt."

Matt didn't see how it would hurt to have his dad come to the game. He was actually excited about the idea—which made him feel a bit guilty. He had often longed to have a father at his games, like everyone else. The dads were always helping out at practice, or managing, or scorekeeping or driving to and from games. Matt's mom had done her share of that stuff, but for some reason it wasn't quite the same.

"I guess it's okay," he told her. "Can you tell him that for me?"

His mother nodded. "Oh, I almost forgot," she said. "I've got some good news today too."

"What is it?" Matt asked.

"I sold the old Baker house over on Wallace. You know, that huge place with the pool and the tennis courts. That's going to be a pretty nice commission."

"Way to go, Mom!" Matt roared, high-fiving her across the table. "Not a bad day for the Hills all around."

Matt had quite a bit of homework to finish up that night. He was taking Spanish for the first

time this year and struggling with it. His accent
was awful. He felt like an idiot every time he
tried to pronounce a word during class. Half the
kids in the class seemed to be of Hispanic heri-
tage, and Matt imagined them rolling around the
aisles laughing at his lame efforts. The language
certainly didn't come naturally to him.

He turned on the computer in his bedroom.
He had a new e-mail from Andrea Thomas. He
hadn't seen much of her since football practice
and school began. They had spent a lot of time
together during the summer, playing pickup
basketball and going for bike rides. Matt liked
Andrea, and he knew the feeling was mutual.
In fact on a couple of long walks in July they
had held hands and Matt had almost worked
up the nerve to kiss her goodnight. But Andrea
had gone to Europe with her parents for the
last couple of weeks of August. And when she
returned, she had jumped right into soccer.
She was a star midfielder for the South Side
girls' team. They didn't have advisory period
together, either, so they only spoke in the
hallway at school and during long telephone
conversations. Matt hadn't realized how much
he'd missed her.

He opened the e-mail. *You made the football*

team! it began. *Nice going, Matt. I knew you would.*

Andrea said the South Side girls' soccer team was looking strong this year. They were playing their first game Thursday night. Could he come and watch?

Thinking about U a lot, it concluded. *Luv, Andrea.*

Matt was alone, but he felt himself blush as he read the e-mail. He hit Reply and wrote back immediately. It was time to tell somebody other than his family about his dad coming back into his life. Somehow, telling Andrea made him feel a little more comfortable about everything, even if it was only in an e-mail.

About an hour into his homework, he looked up to see he had another e-mail. It was Andrea again. *Matt, that's unbelievable news about your dad*, it began. *I just think it's so great of you to be able to forgive like that. If my dad had walked out on me and my mom, I'm not sure I'd be able to do that…You're a special guy. Luv, Andrea.*

Matt felt a glow envelope him as he read the e-mail. He hadn't thought about it that way. But now that Andrea brought it up, he began thinking about Ms. Dawson's theme in advisory that morning. Forgiveness. Being able to forgive somebody when they screwed up, she had said, was an admirable trait to possess. It seemed weird to Matt, though, that the person he was supposedly forgiving was his father.

chapter eight

Between school and football practice, the week shot past in a blur. Eighth grade was proving much more difficult than seventh had been for Matt. Not only was Spanish a tough subject, but he was also still having problems in mathematics, which had never been one of his strengths. And the teachers seemed less inclined to cut second-year students a break. Homework was expected on time, and teachers weren't there to remind you on a regular basis about turning in every assignment. That was elementary school stuff. If you didn't hand something in, you paid the price with an "incomplete" on your record.

As he headed out the door for school on Friday morning, Matt reminded his mom about the game later that day. "It starts at five o'clock at our school, okay?"

"I'll be there with my pom-poms." She smiled.

Matt groaned. He knew his mother had been a cheerleader in high school. But somehow the thought of her dressed in a Stingers cheerleader outfit and turning cartwheels down the side-lines just seemed wrong. Matt hustled down Anderson, toward the big oak where Phil and Jake would be waiting. But when he arrived at the spot, only Jake was there. "Where's Philly?" he asked.

"No idea," replied Jake. "I went to meet him at the store, and his Grandma said he'd gone in early this morning."

They reached school a couple of minutes before the first bell. Matt spied Phil at his locker. "You were here early today," he called across the hall, "What for?"

"Hey, dude, that's strictly confidential foot-ball manager's business." Phil smiled. "I could tell you, but then I'd have to kill you."

Matt laughed.

"Charlie had us all come in early today," Phil explained. "He wanted to get the field lined and every piece of gear ready for the game, so that there won't be any delay getting you guys on the field this afternoon. The kid is ultraserious."

Matt knew that was no exaggeration. Charlie Dougan took his managerial duties seriously. Matt had witnessed that during baseball season when Dougan had spent nearly every Saturday morning of the spring working with him on his hitting. Those hitting sessions had been a huge help to Matt, and he and Charlie had become good friends.

Phil seemed a lot more upbeat today than he had been Monday, but Matt still felt badly for him. They had been talking all summer about going out for football and it didn't seem fair that Phil suddenly had to shelve that dream.

"How is it being a manager, anyway?" Matt asked, a little awkwardly. "I mean, I was surprised that you volunteered."

Phil explained that, on cut-down day, Coach Reynolds had asked him if he still wanted to be part of the team. One way to do that was to be a manager, the coach had said.

"At first, it seemed kind of lame," Phil said. "But I thought about it and decided that I could learn a lot about football just by being around practice and maybe go out for the team again next year."

That was typical Phil—always ready to dig in and do the dirty work. Matt respected the fact that his ego never seemed to get in the way. "Well, Charlie is the right guy to work with," Matt said. "He'll probably end up in the Manager's Hall of Fame, or something." They both laughed.

Matt had wondered whether the football cuts would come between him and Phil. He realized that he should have known better.

Like any game day, school dragged on for Matt. His Spanish quiz was first thing after advisory, and it went all right—he got ten out of fifteen—but the rest of the classes seemed to last forever. Finally, as the bell rang at 3:35 PM, it was time for football.

Matt stuffed his books into his locker and headed for the gym. About twenty players were already in the locker room, and a Billy Talent song was blaring out of Kyle James's portable stereo. In front of each player's stall, uniforms and equipment had been meticulously laid out by the half-dozen busy managers. It looked like a pro-football locker room. As he watched the players already pulling on their pads, football pants, socks and cleats, Matt imagined the team as a medieval army donning its armor before an epic battle.

Matt pulled the crisp white South Side jersey—with the word "Stingers" in maroon block lettering across the chest—over his shoulder pads. He felt absolutely huge in all the pads, the tight white football pants that covered his legs to just above the calves and the black three-quarter-cut cleats he and his mom had picked up on sale at South Vale Sports. He was pumped and felt invincible as he headed out of the locker room with his teammates for the pre-game warm-up.

There was almost an hour until the 5:00 PM kickoff. Kyle James led the entire white-clad South Side team in a couple of laps around the track that ringed the field, followed by a series of calisthenics, before they broke out the footballs. Matt looked across the turf at the visiting North Vale Nuggets. They appeared gigantic in their black helmets and jerseys, with gold piping and lettering. They weren't actually any bigger than South Side, but their colors made them look larger and tougher.

Matt was surprised by how many people were already in the bleachers. There had to be five hundred fans, nearly packing the set of stands that lined the west side of the field. Matt saw his mom, sitting next to Phil's parents. It was cool the Wongs had come, he thought, since their son wasn't even going to play. At the right end of the stands, Matt noticed the large frame of Mr. Jackson, Ricky's dad, standing by the edge of the bleachers, studying the warm-up intently. A few feet past Mr. Jackson, Matt saw his own father, leaning casually against the chain-link fence. Suddenly he felt more nervous than he had before any game in his life.

Coach Reynolds and his assistants rounded up the South Side players and steered them back into the locker room for their pre-game talk. The forty kids filled every spot on the locker room benches, and several players, including Matt, took to one knee on the floor as the coach stood before them.

"Okay, boys," Coach Reynolds began seriously. "This is what we've been practicing for. This is what all the hard work is about. North Vale is going to be a good test for us. All I ask is that you give me every ounce of effort you've got. That's always going to be good enough for me, all right?"

Helmets bobbed up and down. Nobody said a word. The coach continued.

"Now, let's go out there and play some Stingers football!"

The players roared and met in the middle of the floor, their arms extended. "Who are we?" Kyle James yelled.

"We're the Stingers!" his teammates answered back in a collective shout.

"Where are we going?" James screamed.

"All the way!" came the reply.

The team charged out of the locker room door and toward a large rectangular wooden frame that some South Side students had constructed in shop class. Across the opening was a paper banner with the painting of a huge hornet, the Stingers' mascot, on the side facing the crowd. Kyle James led the charge as the Stingers broke through the paper banner, forty players strong. The home crowd erupted.

Matt had never felt so pumped up before any game in any sport. It was kind of weird, since he wasn't likely to get much playing time today. He was penciled in second, behind Nate Brown, in the lone wide receiver's spot on offense. Brown, a senior, would get most of the playing time and the majority of the passes today, he realized.

Still, Matt found himself on the field to begin the game as South Side kicked off to the visitors. He was part of the kick coverage team, so at least he would get a chance to run down the

field and shake some of the jitters early on. The
official blew his whistle, and Ricky Jackson laid
his boot into the ball, sending it on a high arc
down to the twenty-five-yard line, where the
North Vale return man caught it and spun toward
the sidelines. It hadn't been a great boot. Ricky
Jackson had been handling kicking duties as
well as backing up Kyle James at quarterback,
but he wasn't nearly as strong with his leg as
he was with his right arm. Jackson could certainly punt but was weaker on field goals and
kickoffs.

The North Vale return man didn't get far,
however. Matt and Ron Evans both descended
upon him at the thirty-five-yard line, Matt wrapping his arms around the Nugget player's waist
and Evans taking his legs. It was a terrific hit to
start the ball game. The crowd roared, and Matt
came off the field feeling as alive as he could
ever remember.

That play seemed to set the tone for the game
too. North Vale was simply no match for the
Stingers. Kyle James used a combination of deft
handoffs and short accurate passes to pick apart
the Nuggets' defense, with Nate Brown on the
receiving end of most throws. Meanwhile, the
Evans twins anchored the South Side defense,

attacking ball carriers and pass receivers with redheaded abandon.

By halftime it was 28–7 for South Side. At the end of three quarters, the Stingers led 35–7. Coach Reynolds began emptying his bench. "Jackson, take over for James at quarterback," he barked. "Hill, go in for Brown at receiver."

Matt had expected Jackson to get some quarterbacking time well before then. He had been looking good in practice, particularly with his ability to throw deep. Although he wasn't quite as experienced or patient as Kyle James, he certainly had a better arm. But James, a ninth-grader, was the starter. Coach Reynolds had made that perfectly clear to everybody from the beginning.

In the first huddle, Jackson turned to Matt. "We're going deep fly, twenty-five yards. Can you beat your man?" Matt nodded, but at the same time he honestly had no idea if he could beat his man. This was his first time on the field for an offensive series. The huddle broke and the teams went to the line. Jackson started the snap count, but his cadence was slightly different than James's, and center Steve Donnelly pulled up early. The referee threw a flag. It was an illegal procedure call.

Jackson glanced toward the sidelines. His father had thrown his maroon hat to the ground in disgust. People in the stands were staring at the large man warily.

"Let's try the same thing again," Ricky said, turning to the huddle. "This time, on two. Everybody know the count?"

Heads nodded all around. This time, Donnelly did not pull up early. Jackson took the snap and dropped back. Meanwhile, Matt had fired off the line, getting a full step on his man. He reached the twenty-five-yard mark in about three seconds. The ball was headed his way, and it was a perfect throw. He reached up with his right hand. But as he shot up his left to gather in the pass, the football bounced away. He had dropped what should have been an easy catch. Matt glanced back at Jackson. The young quarterback wasn't even looking down the field, though. His eyes were glued to the sidelines where his father once again appeared furious.

Matt felt horrible, but not just for himself. He knew he would catch passes and drop passes during his football career—that simply went with the position of receiver. He felt badly for Jackson, who was clearly feeling the pressure from his father. The Stingers punted the ball, one of the few times all game that they hadn't scored. Matt and his offensive teammates returned to the sidelines.

By the time South Side got the ball back, it was mid-fourth quarter as North Vale had rallied against the Stingers' backup defense and scored a touchdown to make it 35–14. Jackson put his helmet on to return to the field, but Coach Reynolds stopped him. "Vickers is going in for this series," he said.

Jackson was clearly disappointed. Keith Vickers was the third-strong quarterback and backup receiver. Jackson had gotten only one series and already Coach was pulling him for the third-stringer. As Matt headed out to the field, he couldn't help but feel responsible. After all, he had dropped a nice pass.

There was a sudden commotion on the sidelines. When Vickers came out to take the snap, Jackson's dad had turned his back and stomped away, slamming the chain-link gate as he left the area. A few people in the stands were snickering at him. Matt noticed his father standing nearby, calmly sipping on a coffee. He felt sorry for Ricky.

A few minutes later, the game was over. South Side had won 42–14, an easy victory.

Matt had managed to catch one pass, a ten-yard
out pattern that was part of a nice touchdown
drive engineered by Keith Vickers. He had also
dropped another ball when he heard a North Vale
linebacker thundering up behind him. Matt knew
that if he wanted to be a receiver he had to focus
on the football and not worry about getting hit.
But that was much easier said than done.

All in all, though, it had been a great start
to the football season, both for South Side and
for Matt. The locker room was upbeat, tunes
cranked and players celebrating the big win.
Coach Reynolds motioned to Kyle James to turn
off the stereo.

"Nice game, guys," the coach said, a bigger
smile on his face than Matt had seen before. "I'm
really pleased with most of what I saw today, and
the things I wasn't pleased with we can work to
correct. Most of all, I'm happy with the effort. It
was a good win. Let's come back Monday and
get ready for Central."

The locker room din quickly rose again as
Coach Reynolds made his way over to Ricky
Jackson's stall. The coach motioned to Jackson
to follow him into his office in the hallway,
just off the locker room. Coach closed the door
behind them.

"Wonder what's going on in there?" Ron Evans whispered, putting words to what just about everybody was thinking.

The conversation soon swung to other more pressing matters, such as who caught the most passes, which cheerleader was the best-looking and, inevitably, to the Central Wildcats next week. It would be a road game, the Stingers' first of the season, and it would be tough. Central was ranked number one in the league and in the entire region. South Side would get a major test in its next game.

Matt showered and dressed before heading out the locker room door. He had promised his mother he'd come right home so the two could go out for pizza and a movie. But he discovered he had a visitor waiting.

"Hi, Matt, nice game." It was his father.

Once again, Matt felt awkward.

"Um, thanks," he said, looking down. "I dropped a few I should have caught, but we kicked them pretty good."

"You sure did," his dad said, flashing a smile. "And I thought you did just great, especially for your first real football game. That opening tackle was terrific."

Matt blushed. His father had obviously

watched the game closely to know that he had been in on that tackle. It was the play that Matt had been most proud of today too.

"Anyway, I just thought I'd come and say hello," his father said. "I know you and your mom are busy tonight. But I'll call you and maybe we can get together this week sometime. How does that sound?"

"Sure," Matt said. "That sounds good."

His father waved as he headed toward his black SUV parked on Anderson, just outside the school lot. It still felt strange to Matt, this idea of having a dad in his life. Strange, but at the same time, kind of nice too.

chapter nine

The first thing Matt noticed the next morning was how sore his body felt. It was the difference between practicing and having played full speed in the game the previous afternoon. Everything was just one more notch up on the intensity scale, including the day-after stiffness he was now experiencing.

He had slept well and was happy that he had a free Saturday. No practice today, just the regular game of pickup hoops at Anderson Park with the guys. Matt loved organized sports, but it was also nice to get a day to just kick back, have a few laughs and enjoy himself with his best friends.

Jake and Phil knocked on his front door about 10:00 AM and the three of them headed over to the park, where they met up with Amar Sunir, another good buddy and a teammate on the South Side basketball squad. It was a slightly overcast day with a hint of autumn cool in the air, not nice enough, obviously, to draw anybody else here for an outdoor game. Just as well. Matt and his buddies loved these two-on-two matchups.

They shot for teams, with Matt and Phil pairing up and Jake and Amar playing together. It was a difficult matchup for Matt and Phil against the bigger and more athletic duo. But they held their own, splitting the first two games to eleven by ones.

"Hey, Matt," Phil asked during a water break before the deciding game. "Who was that guy you were talking to last night after the game—a college recruiter or something?"

Matt laughed. "I wish," he said.

He guessed it was time he told his friends about his father. Besides his mom and Mark, Andrea was the only person who knew about the big change in his life so far. And Matt knew Andrea hadn't told anybody about it. For some reason—he didn't quite know why—he had asked her not to.

"That's wild," Phil said after Matt finished, his eyes wide at the news.

"For sure," added Jake.

Matt instantly felt better, now that he had told his friends. They had pretty much shared everything growing up. Still, Matt had been the only one of the four who hadn't had a dad around. Now, suddenly, he did. It was kind of a strange feeling: as if his identity had been altered.

"It's been kind of bizarre," Matt admitted to his friends as he took a warm-up shot.

"Bizarre?" Phil said. "You want to know what's bizarre? How about Ricky Jackson's dad? Do you guys know what happened after the game last night?"

Matt hadn't heard a thing.

"I was right there by the locker room door, so I heard it kind of by accident," Phil continued. "Jackson's old man freaked out on Coach. He was yelling at him, telling Coach his kid should be starting instead of Kyle. He said Ricky was by far the best football player on the entire team and was getting cheated out of playing time because the South Side coaches don't like the family."

Matt was surprised, but not completely. He knew Jackson's dad had a temper. He had seen it in action during the basketball season after Ricky's older brother, Grant, had been suspended for shoplifting.

"Then he really went off," Phil said. "He told Coach Reynolds that if Ricky had some decent receivers, he'd be all-district and that it was a joke that he wasn't starting. He said none of you guys can run a route or catch a ball. It was brutal."

Matt's ears burned. He didn't have to be a mind reader to know that Jackson's dad didn't like it when any of his son's passes were dropped, even in a practice drill. But Matt didn't like the idea of anybody, even a parent, criticizing him like that.

"That's why Coach called Ricky into his office after the game," Phil said. "I was watching during that series he played, and before every huddle, Ricky was looking toward his dad on the sidelines. Coach thinks Ricky's dad is calling in plays to him."

Now that was strange. Matt knew Jackson's dad was demanding and a control freak, but this was beyond anything he had imagined. But now it made more sense. No wonder Ricky looked to the sidelines before and after every play.

Matt imagined being in Jackson's situation. It was difficult enough to listen to your coaches and to pay attention to the plays your team had called let alone take directions from your dad on the field too.

The four friends resumed their game of two-on-two. Matt and Phil put up a good effort, but in the third game, the combined height and athleticism of Jake and Amar won out. Jake finished off the game with a spinning drive that he banked in for the winning layup.

"Take that, football boys," Jake laughed as he and Amar high-fived. Matt had wondered whether the fact he and Phil had decided to go out for football would drive a wedge between them and the other two, but it was obvious it hadn't.

Matt spent the rest of the weekend catching up on homework and raking the leaves that had already begun to fall on their yard. On Sunday, Mark drove down from Eton for a visit. He hadn't been home since before football practice began and it was good to see him.

Before supper, Mark asked Matt if he wanted to shoot some hoops at Anderson. "Sure," Matt said. "But watch out. I might tackle you. I'm in football season now."

They walked slowly to the park with basketballs in hand. Matt could tell Mark wanted to discuss something serious with him because there was no small talk or joking as they approached the park.

"He called me the other day again," Mark said, finally.

"You mean Dad?" Matt said. "Yeah, he came to my football game."

Matt couldn't help notice Mark's brow furrow.

"I told him that I don't want to see him," Mark said.

Silence. The brothers didn't speak for several seconds.

"How come?" Matt finally asked.

"I guess it's different for you," Mark said, slowly. "I mean, you were just a baby, basically, when he left. But I wasn't. It was rough. Mom was a wreck. And he just took off. Before he left, he told me why. He said he had gotten involved with another woman and that Mom couldn't forgive him for that. So he just left. He said it was the best thing for everybody.

"But you know what? It wasn't the best thing for me or you, or even Mom. I wanted a dad. I didn't have one. He just left, and I'll never forgive him for that."

It was all spilling out quickly, like it had been bottled up inside Mark for years just waiting to erupt. Matt slowly digested what he had just heard. He and Mark had never talked so openly about their mom and dad before. He wondered why not.

They shot baskets in silence for a few minutes. Neither of them tried to start a game of one-on-one. They were both in deep thought, with only the sound of the basketballs bouncing off the pavement and clanging on the rim interrupting the quiet.

"Are you pissed at me?" Matt finally asked. "I mean, for seeing him?"

Mark shook his head. "No, man," he said. "You do what you think is right. I just know that I can't see him right now. Maybe not ever."

They walked back toward the house, again mostly in silence. Once they walked through the front door, they didn't mention their father again. Mark and Matt sat down to a roast beef and mashed potato dinner with Mom, just as they had on many a Sunday evening. They talked about football and Mark's job and his new girlfriend Serena and even the weather. The subject of their father didn't come up again that night.

chapter ten

Only a dozen blocks separated the South Side campus from rival Central Middle School, but Coach Reynolds wasn't asking his players to walk to their Friday afternoon game. Coach wanted the boys to "save their legs," so he had ordered up two long yellow school buses to transport the team and all its gear over to the Wildcats' home field.

Matt thought the players could have easily made the walk to Central. The managers were another story, however. Although the Stingers were already dressed in their full uniforms for the bus ride, Charlie, Phil and the rest of the managers struggled onto the bus with several huge black duffel bags full of footballs, tape, clipboards, video equipment and water bottles.

"Don't stand there boys," Coach Reynolds yelled at his players. "Help out with the bags. We're all teammates here."

Embarrassed, Matt jumped up to give Phil a hand. Ricky also got up quickly to help Charlie. Matt was surprised. Ricky seemed nicer than his older brother Grant had been last basketball season. Matt was pretty confi-dent Grant had never helped a team manager in his life.

It was nearly four thirty by the time the Stingers took to the neatly manicured, dark green turf of Central Middle School. The booster club at Central focused heavily on football and everything at the Wildcats' home field was top-notch. The white stands sat at least six hundred people, and the turf was expertly lined and crowned with the giant logo of a snarling Wildcat at midfield.

Central was ranked number one in both the league and the district. The Wildcats had one of the best ninth-grade running backs in the entire region in bruising Lionel Pierce, whom the newspapers were already touting as possessing major college potential. Central's entire offense was built around Pierce, who

had simply run through other teams as an
eighth-grader. He also dominated the other
side of the ball for the Wildcats as a hard-hit-
ting middle linebacker.

The game began well for South Side. They
received the opening kickoff and drove all the
way for a touchdown on the first possession,
with Kyle James throwing a seven-yard pass to
Nate Brown for the major. The way Brown had
beaten his man and cradled the ball so smoothly
in his hands as he crossed into the end zone made
Matt wish he was half as good a football player
as the slender ninth-grader.

But despite the solid start, the Stingers'
offense had stalled following that drive. The only
saving grace for South Side was that Central was
having problems scoring too. Even though the
Wildcats were marching up and down the field
with relative ease, they hadn't been able to punch
the ball into the end zone by the half. Lionel
Pierce had come close, turning in an electrifying
twenty-five-yard run early in the second quarter,
but the Central star had been drilled by Ronnie
Evans and fumbled the football. Reggie Evans
had recovered it, all smiles and freckles as he
lifted his helmeted head off the turf.

"Good half," Coach Reynolds said in the

locker room at the intermission. "We've got a seven-o lead. I would have preferred to be up by fourteen or twenty-one, but we are up. Keep that in mind. You guys are in control. Outplay them this half and we've got a mighty sweet win here."

Matt was fired up as he took to the field to begin the second half. The Stingers were kicking off, and he was making only his second appearance of the game with the kick coverage team.

Ricky Jackson laid his right boot into the ball. But it was a wobbly kick, traveling perhaps thirty yards before coming down in front of a surprised Lionel Pierce. The short kick also caught the Stingers' coverage team off guard. As he zeroed in on the bullish Pierce, Matt lunged for the Central back and tried to wrap his arms around his opponent's waist. But Pierce was ready. He straight-armed Matt, deflecting the tackle. As Matt looked up from the ground, he saw Pierce thundering alone toward the Stingers' end zone.

The crowd went crazy. Coach Reynolds fumed on the sidelines, squeezing his clipboard and closing his eyes. This wasn't the kind of start to the second half that the South Side coach had hoped for.

The rest of the half was fairly even—a little surprising considering the Stingers weren't even ranked in the district and were playing on the Wildcats' field. But with five minutes remaining, Central managed to put together a drive. Led by the continued pounding of Lionel Pierce, the Wildcats drove the ball to the Stingers' twenty-yard line before the possession stalled. On its final down, Central sent out its field-goal unit.

Once again it was Pierce doing the damage. The ninth-grader not only ran the ball, he also kicked it for the Wildcats. The roughly thirty-yard kick was just a chip shot for Pierce's powerful right leg. The football split the uprights and Central had a 10–7 lead.

Coach Reynolds called a time-out. He motioned for the entire team to gather around him on the sidelines. Matt strained to hear the coach's words from the back row.

"Okay, people," the coach said calmly. "We've played a good game here. We've had a real solid effort. Now we just need one more drive from you guys.

"Central is going to be playing prevent here. They're not going to give up the deep one. We've got plenty of time. Kyle, just chip away on this drive, okay?"

Kyle James nodded. Despite the intensity of the moment, Matt could sense a quiet confidence in the gray eyes of the ninth-grade quarterback. "Let's go, boys," James said, stretching his left hand out in the middle of his teammates. "One, two, three—Stingers!"

The first-string offense ran onto the field. Matt, as usual, watched from the sidelines as Nate Brown lined up at wide receiver. Matt was pretty sure everybody watching the game knew that the ball was going to Brown on this drive. He was easily the Stingers' top pass-catching threat.

Central's defense must have been thinking the same thing. On first down, Brown streaked upfield ten yards before cutting quickly outside. Lionel Pierce, playing middle linebacker, followed Brown through the backfield along his down-and-out route. He obviously felt the ball was going to the Stingers' best receiver too.

Kyle James rolled out to the right, the same side as Brown was cutting. He cocked his left arm and began to pass the ball to his favorite target. But at the last second, he tucked it under his arm and cut directly upfield. The fake seemed to catch the entire Wildcats team by surprise because the middle of the field was wide open.

Pierce had committed to covering Brown, and James easily scampered for fifteen yards and a first down.

The Stingers now had the ball at midfield with more than three minutes left on the clock. They broke their huddle quickly, with James dropping back about five yards behind center Steve Donnelly in a shotgun formation. The long snap came back to the South Side quarterback, who again looked downfield at Nate Brown who was steaming down the right sidelines. Once again, however, it was a decoy. James whirled and threw to Steve Chase, the halfback who normally didn't do much in the offense except block. Chase had slipped quietly out of the backfield and run ten yards up the middle. He caught the pass and was tackled by a swarm of Wildcat defenders. The Stingers had another first down.

Matt could hardly contain himself on the sidelines. He wasn't playing, but it was almost more exciting to watch the end of this game. It was like some of those last-minute NFL cliffhangers that had mesmerized him on Sunday afternoons. The game was down to the wire.

The next two downs didn't go as well for the Stingers. James was sacked for a one-yard loss, and then Steve Chase dropped an easy seven-yard pass that he should have caught. That left third down with the Stingers desperately needing to keep the drive alive.

The large Central crowd was cheering, "DeeFence! DeeFence!" as the Stingers broke their huddle. Once again, James dropped back into the shotgun. He took the snap, began to roll to the right, but then he reversed his field and went left, away from his wall of blockers. Three Central defenders, including Pierce, were furiously bearing down on the South Side quarterback, who by now was on a dead run toward the left sidelines.

Just as it appeared certain that James was going to be caught by his pursuers for a huge loss, his left arm flashed forward. He had managed to get away a long pass down the left sidelines. The ball was headed on a high spiral toward Brown and the Wildcat defensive back who was still covering him tightly.

The two players went up for the ball and crashed violently into one another in midair. Matt and his teammates could hear the collision all the way over on the far sidelines. The ball tipped off Nate Brown's fingers, hung delicately in the air for what seemed like a second, and then it fell toward the ground. But the Stingers' receiver somehow managed to snake his left hand around the ball as he descended to the turf. Brown had made an unbelievable one-handed catch to move the Stingers to the Central fifteen-yard line.

The South Side bench was going crazy over the circus catch. But their celebration was short-lived. Although Brown had made a spectacular play, he had also injured himself. He was still lying on his back on the field as the officials spotted the ball for the next play.

Coach Reynolds sent Matt, Phil and Charlie onto the field to help Nate. It was his right ankle. The ninth-grader had twisted it as he crashed to the ground. The managers each grabbed an arm and Matt helped hoist Brown as they maneuvered the star receiver to the sidelines.

There were less than two minutes left on the clock now, and Coach Reynolds again called a time-out. "Kyle," he said, looking at his quarterback, "if we can get this in the end zone, it's our game."

James nodded, the sweat dripping from the portions of his face visible inside his helmet. "I want to run the ball—quarterback keeps—for the next two downs," Coach continued. "Keep the ball in the middle in case we need to go for a field goal."

Once again, the Stingers trotted onto the turf. Central's defense was already lined up and waiting. On first down, James stumbled slightly as he took the snap from Steve Donnelly. Pierce smelled the play right away and leveled James behind the line of scrimmage. South Side had lost a yard. It was second down, and the clock was ticking.

The next play wasn't much better. James took the snap and tried to bull his way up the middle. But he wasn't going anywhere against the swarming Central defense. He had gained just over a yard. It was third down, and Coach Reynolds had seen enough. "Time-out!" he shouted.

There were thirty seconds left on the clock as the players once again headed to the side-lines. "We need to go for a field goal on this play," Coach told the players. "If we try to score again, we might run out the clock before we get a chance to kick. The field goal's the way to go, especially with Nate out."

Matt looked over at Brown, who by now had a large ice bag taped to his right ankle. Assistant coach Kevin Stone interrupted his thoughts.

"Hill, you're holding," Stone reminded him.

Matt hadn't immediately realized what Brown's injury meant. Of course he would be holding for this kick. Nate was the first-string holder and he was Nate's backup. Matt quickly pulled on his helmet, did up the chin strap and listened intently.

"It's not a long kick," Coach Reynolds said to Ricky Jackson, who had been warming up by booting a ball into a practice net on the sidelines. "You've made a million of these in practice, son."

Ricky nodded confidently at the coach. The players once again broke their sideline huddle, heading onto the field for the game-deciding play. Matt felt pretty confident. He had held the ball for plenty of field-goal attempts since practice began a month ago. Just as long as he got a good snap from Donnelly…

Matt's thoughts were broken in the huddle by Ricky Jackson. "Guys, we're going for the win," he said, looking around at his teammates. "Hill, when you get the snap, lateral it to me. Then head for the shallow end zone, right side. I'll get it to you, okay? Just catch it."

"But Coach said—" Once again Matt was interrupted.

"I'm changing the call," Jackson said. "Let's go. On two."

The South Side players broke their huddle and lined up in field-goal formation. Matt, now nervous, waited for the ball to be snapped by Steve Donnelly. The snap came, right on target. Matt caught it and saw Ricky Jackson run toward him as if he was going to kick the ball. As Jackson had directed in the huddle, Matt did not place the ball down for the field goal. Instead he lateraled it to the backup quarterback and headed for the end zone.

Matt was wide-open as he crossed the goal line. He looked back for the pass but instantly knew it wasn't coming. Lionel Pierce had once again guessed the Stingers' play from his middle linebacker position. The Wildcat star had streaked around the line of blockers and leveled Ricky Jackson before he could even raise his right arm to pass. As Matt looked backward, Pierce's imposing figure was still prone on top of the dejected Jackson.

Matt glanced across the field at the South Side bench. Coach Reynolds had thrown his clipboard to the ground in disgust. The Stingers had lost the game 10–7 and, just as the coach had feared, the clock had run out before South Side could re-huddle. It was not going to be a happy bus ride home.

The players from both teams shook hands, and the Stingers headed for the yellow school buses that had brought them there. One by one, the dejected South Side players filed into their seats. Matt was on the same bus with Ricky Jackson, Nate Brown and Kyle James. He noticed Coach Reynolds step into the front of the other bus and deliver a few words to the players. Then the coach came over to their bus.

"No meeting today, guys," he said, calmer than Matt would have predicted. "We'll hash this one out Monday at practice. Good effort."

The coach paused before taking his seat at the front of the bus, directly behind the driver. "Hill and Jackson," he said, looking at the middle of the vehicle where Matt and Ricky sat a couple of seats apart. "I want to talk to you guys when we get back to the school."

Matt gulped. He didn't have to be a psychic to know what that meeting was going to be about. Going for a touchdown on a fake field goal directly against the coach's orders had cost the Stingers a huge tie. Matt wasn't looking forward to this meeting at all.

The bus ride back to South Side took just a

couple of minutes. Matt wished it could last a lot longer. He suspected the experience at the other end wasn't going to be pleasant, and he was right.

He and Ricky Jackson followed the coach to his office adjacent to the locker room. "Have a seat, boys," Coach Reynolds said.

The coach cleared his throat and looked directly at the players with his steely eyes. "Let's get something straight right now," he said, his voice firm and cold. "I am the coach of this football team. Period! When I call a play, I want that play run. I don't want another play run. Do you guys understand?"

Both players nodded solemnly. Neither said a word.

"Then why the heck did you try that fake field goal? That cost us the game. Do you guys realize that?"

Again, both Matt and Ricky nodded.

"I can't let this go without a punishment," the coach continued. "It wouldn't be fair to the other kids on the team. They worked hard all game; they deserved better than this. So I am suspending you both for next week's game against Churchill. You will practice, but you won't play. You'll both be third-string for the week and have to earn back your spots in the depth chart."

Matt was reeling. All he had done was follow his quarterback's call in the huddle. He had known that they should have run the play Coach had called on the sidelines, but what was he supposed to do in the situation? The Stingers had no time-outs left. The clock was winding down. Matt had simply done the only thing he possibly could in what had been an impossible situation.

He was just about to defend himself when he heard the voice beside him. "Coach, I have to say something," Ricky said slowly, looking over at him. "It wasn't Matt's fault. I changed the play in the huddle. I told him I was the quarterback and it was my call. He shouldn't be suspended too."

Coach Reynolds mulled this over for a second and then spoke, "Okay, Hill. You can go now. I'm going to let you off with a warning this time."

Relief welled up inside Matt. "Jackson, we have more to talk about," the coach continued. "You stick around."

Matt heard the coach begin to speak to Jackson again as he closed the door to the office and headed out of the locker room. On one hand, he felt sorry for Ricky. Not only was he dealing with the coach, but his dad was also going to be steamed when he found out about the suspension.

On the other hand, Matt was also angry with Ricky. He had got him into trouble with the coach and for what? Because he wanted to be the big hero with the game-winning play? He resented Jackson for putting him in that awkward position.

As he left the quiet locker room, Matt noticed his father's dark SUV parked on Anderson Crescent, across from the school. His dad waved from the driver's seat and opened the door. "Hey, Matt," he said gently. "Tough one to lose."

"Yeah, it sure was," Matt replied. "We really messed up with that fake field goal at the end."

Matt's dad didn't say anything about the play. "Hey, chalk it up to experience, kid," he said. "It's just a game, right?"

Matt nodded. He climbed in the passenger seat and smiled at his father. He was right. It was just a game. But Matt was pretty sure Ricky's dad wouldn't be looking at things in quite the same way.

chapter eleven

The buzz in the locker room Monday afternoon was obvious as Matt and his teammates got ready for practice.

"Did you hear about Jackson?" Reggie Evans said, eyeing Matt. "He's suspended for two games for that play he called against Central. Coach is steamed."

"So's Jackson's dad," interjected Kyle James. "I wouldn't have wanted to be that kid on the weekend."

Almost everyone laughed at Kyle's remark. The entire school seemed to know that Ricky's father had a temper and that he was always getting into fights with coaches and other parents. Matt wasn't laughing, however. He wondered what had happened to Jackson over the weekend.

His dad was so crazy about football and, it seemed, just crazy, period.

Matt grabbed his helmet and headed to the field. He was looking forward to running and hitting and blowing off some steam. He had been stewing all weekend about what had happened at the end of the Central game, wondering what else he could have done about it. He had talked to his mom and she was glad he wasn't suspended. But neither she nor anybody else had any answers about how he could have handled the situation differently.

Matt had gotten ready so quickly that he was surprised to see he wasn't the first South Side player on the field. Down at the far end of the turf, a short kid wearing a yellow practice jersey was booting balls through the uprights. And funny enough, Phil Wong was holding for him.

Matt approached the pair, wondering who this new kicker was. He hadn't thought much about it, but it made sense that Coach would audition somebody as a placekicker since Jackson was suspended. Jackson hadn't been doing a great job kicking over the first two games, anyway.

Phil had assembled a large bucket of footballs and was grabbing them one by one for the new player to boot. The kid was good. He was split-ting the uprights on these twenty-five-yarders with almost every kick.

"Mattster!" Phil grinned as his friend approached. "What do you think of our new kicker?"

The player in the yellow jersey turned slowly. Matt recognized him now. It was Charlie Dougan. He was wearing a smile so wide that it shone through the bars on his helmet faceguard.

"Hey, Charlie," Matt said. "I didn't know you kicked."

Matt was stunned to see Dougan in a uni-form. Matt knew that he'd had his leg brace removed, but he didn't realize that Dougan was now cleared to play sports.

"I'm just messing around," Charlie said, a little nervously. "Coach told me he'd be trying out some new kickers today. I thought I'd give it a shot."

Phil interjected. "He's good, man. Charlie's got range and he's accurate."

"Awesome," Matt said. "Good luck, Doogie. You're looking good so far."

Charlie went back to his practice, lofting foot-balls high through the goalposts. Matt knew from his work with Dougan on the pitching machine the previous baseball season that Charlie's technique would eventually be flawless and that he would outwork anybody. Charlie Dougan was the kind of kid who approached tasks ultraseriously. Matt knew he loved sports. It was nice to see him in a uniform.

By now, most of the South Side players were on the field. Coach Reynolds blew his whistle and summoned everybody to midfield. The players took one knee, resting their helmets on the grass beside them.

"Okay, guys," the coach began. "We all know what happened at the end of the Central game. But what I don't understand is why it happened."

Silence all around.

"I told the kids who were involved that I am the coach and I call the plays," Coach Reynolds continued. "Is that clear to everybody else out here?"

Heads nodded.

"Okay, then. You should all know that Ricky Jackson has been suspended for two games for not listening to instructions at Central. It wasn't that he messed up. I can handle mistakes. But I will not tolerate players ignoring my directions. Just so you

know, Ricky will be practicing with us for the
next two weeks but not playing."

The players looked around. Jackson wasn't
on the field. Matt wondered why.

"Because of Jackson's suspension, we are
also now looking for a placekicker," the coach
continued. "So at the end of practice today, I
want any of you interested in that job to come
see me. We'll have a little try-out."

Matt wasn't interested in kicking, but he
was curious to see how Charlie Dougan would
do up against other players. After practice had
finished, he took a seat on the sidelines with a
handful of others to watch the group of four kids
assembled in front of Coach Reynolds.

Both the Evans twins were trying out, and
so was Kyle James, the team's starting quarterback. Charlie was facing some stiff competition, Matt thought. This was going to be
interesting,

"Hill," yelled the coach, "I need somebody to
hold for these guys. Thanks for volunteering."

Matt hadn't exactly volunteered, but he didn't
mind. He sprang off his seat on the sidelines and
took up a position a few yards behind Phil, who
would be snapping footballs to him.

The quartet of placekicking hopefuls began

with ten-yard fieldgoal attempts from the middle of the field and at angles from both sides. These were just chip shots, and only Reggie Evans had trouble with one of his kicks, sending it wide left.

Coach Reynolds had all the players move back ten yards. Now it would get interesting. Charlie Dougan went first. After the snap came back to Matt, Dougan calmly stepped into the ball with his right foot. The football split the uprights perfectly, with plenty of distance to spare.

"Nice boot, Charlie," Coach Reynolds said.

Only Dougan, Ron Evans and Kyle James were able to hit with any consistency from twenty yards. Coach Reynolds then moved those three back to the thirty-yard line. This was serious distance for a middle-school kicker, Matt thought. He wondered if any of them would be able to make it from here.

James went first this time. The Stingers' quarterback had plenty of leg strength, but he wasn't accurate from this distance, pulling two of his three attempts badly wide. Evans was next, but this was clearly out of his range. The redheaded linebacker was short by at least five yards on each of his attempts, while his twin brother Reggie snickered from the sidelines.

That left Charlie Dougan. Matt wondered what was going through the head of the ninth-grader. Here was a kid who had picked up towels and equipment and basically babysat others through baseball and football seasons. Now he was actually getting a shot at playing. Matt couldn't help but think that he'd be nervous in this situation if it were him trying out in front of the coach and other players.

But if Charlie was nervous, he certainly wasn't showing it. On each of his three attempts, he stepped up calmly to the ball and rocketed it through the middle of the uprights. They were perfect field goals, still with distance to spare even at thirty yards.

"I think we've found our kicker," said Coach Reynolds. "And we've lost one heckuva man-ager."

Charlie beamed through his helmet as he high-fived Phil and Matt. The other kicker can didates also came over to congratulate Dougan. They all felt good for him.

Matt, Phil and Charlie walked toward the locker room together. "This is gonna seem weird," Dougan said, pulling off his helmet. "I'm used to cleaning up the messes, not making them."

Matt laughed. "Hey, where did that leg come from?" he asked. "I mean, you wore that big brace for so long. How can you just come out and boot it like that?"

Charlie smiled. He had suffered from Perthes' disease, a condition where not enough blood was reaching his hip, and he had worn a bulky brace on his left leg for about a year. He had expected to wear the brace for another year, but doctors had told him late this summer that his condition had improved enough to remove it early.

"My right leg got stronger from helping the left one out all the time when it was in the brace," Dougan said. "A fringe benefit for me, I guess."

They had just turned the corner toward the locker room when they heard the yelling coming from the doorway. Up ahead was Coach Reynolds. Doing all the yelling was Mr. Jackson, who was standing in front of his silent son Ricky.

"First you suspend him and now you got a gimp taking over his job?" Mr. Jackson was red-faced as he spat the words out at Coach Reynolds. "You're not going to get away with this crap."

With that, Ricky's dad stormed off, pulling

his son along with him. Coach Reynolds headed straight into the locker room. Matt and Phil looked at each other and then at Charlie. The word *gimp* was still hanging in the air like a dark cloud.

"Don't worry about it," Matt said quietly. "The guy's a jerk. I mean, I kind of feel sorry for Ricky. He doesn't seem like a bad kid."

"I'm not worried," Charlie replied, trying to sound like he would have no problem shrugging it off. Still, Matt could tell that a little of the wind had been taken out of his sails.

"Hey, guys," Phil interjected. "Why don't you come over to the store tonight and we can watch *Monday Night Football*?"

"Sounds good," Matt said. "Count me in."

"Me too," said Charlie.

After a quiet dinner with his mom that night, Matt jumped on his bike and pedaled the eight blocks to Wong's Grocery, the tiny corner store that Phil's grandmother had operated for decades. He pulled his bike up to the black iron rack at the front of the store. The lights were glowing softly inside, and through the store's front window Matt could see Phil's grandmother behind the counter. He opened the door with the 7-Up logo on the wide white handle and stepped inside. The smell of penny candy from the dual aisles near the counter hit him immediately. It was a smell that brought back memories of days spent with Phil in the store, playing video games, watching baseball on TV and just hanging out. It was a good smell, Matt thought.

"Hello, Matt," Phil's grandmother beamed, rushing around the counter to give him a hug. "My Lucky Boy!"

Matt felt his cheeks growing red. Phil's grandmother had nicknamed him "Lucky Boy" years ago. Matt wasn't sure what it meant, exactly—whether he was a lucky boy himself or whether he was some sort of good-luck charm for Phil's grandmother. Either way, it made him feel warm inside.

"Hey, Mattster," Phil said, strolling out from the back room with Charlie Dougan. "Come on back, the game's just getting started."

Matt smiled at Phil's grandmother and passed through the red curtain into the back room, which was sort of a combination living room and bedroom. This was where Phil's grandmother lived. But she had always opened it up to Phil and his friends as a place to hang out. Meanwhile, the boys helped her around the store with odd jobs whenever she needed it.

The three boys munched on potato chips and chocolate milk as they watched the *Monday Night Football* game between Seattle and New England. Matt marveled at the size and speed of these NFL players. By comparison, middle school players were shrimps who moved in slow motion.

"We celebrate tonight," exclaimed Phil's grandmother, carrying a small chocolate cake into the back room and laying it in front of the boys. In the middle of the cake sat a plastic football figure, frozen in a kicking motion. "This is Charlie's special day."

Charlie's eyes grew wide as he realized the cake was for him. Phil and his grandma had cooked up a surprise to honor Charlie for becoming the new South Side placekicker.

"Cool," Charlie said, eyeing Phil and his grandmother. "And thanks. This is nice."

Matt was proud of Charlie Dougan. The kid had fought through a serious leg disease and had worked hard to earn a spot on the team. But he also felt proud of Phil. Here was a guy who wanted to play football badly too. Others would have been choked to see the manager get a spot on the team ahead of them. But not Phil. Matt wasn't exactly surprised to see his buddy act so unselfishly. He had known Phil for a long, long time. But as he looked at the smile on Charlie's face, he didn't know if he'd ever been happier to call Philip David Wong a friend.

chapter twelve

Practice that week was tough. South Side had a big home game against the Churchill Bulldogs on Friday night, and the Stingers couldn't afford a loss if they wanted to stay in the hunt for the league title and a spot in the playoffs. Not after that devastating last-minute loss to the Central Wildcats the week before.

Nate Brown was limping badly through much of the week, favoring the right ankle he had twisted late in the game against the Wildcats. That meant Matt got most of the practice reps at wide receiver. He estimated that he'd run a hundred routes with first-string quarterback Kyle James during the last few days. The timing between the two of them had improved as a result. Matt was feeling more and more confident as the week progressed.

As Ricky Jackson was still on suspension, Keith Vickers, normally the third-string quarterback, had been elevated to the backup role behind James. Jackson stood solemnly on the sidelines for most of practice that week, getting in only a handful of reps behind James and Vickers.

Matt felt sorry for Jackson. He knew the kid was under a lot of pressure from his father and that his older brother, Grant, had a hair-trigger temper. He wondered what it must be like living in their house with Jackson's dad on the warpath. Ricky hadn't smiled too much this week, Matt noticed. No matter how talented the kid was, Matt didn't think he'd ever want to trade places with him.

On Thursday night, Matt's mom had a house to show. So the two of them went out to Classico's for a pizza before she had to leave for work. With football, school and his dad suddenly emerging in his life, Matt hadn't had as much one-on-one time with his mother through August and September. It was nice to get a chance to sneak away for a quiet dinner in a booth at the back of the neighborhood restaurant.

"How's football?" Mom asked as she bit into a slice of pizza.

"Pretty good," Matt replied. "You remember Charlie Dougan, right?"

"You mean the boy with the brace on his leg?" she said. "Yes, he helped you with your batting last spring. Isn't he a manager with the football team too?"

"Not anymore," Matt said. "He's our kicker now." Then he launched into the story of how Charlie had tried out the day before to replace Ricky on field goals.

"That's terrific for Charlie," his mom said before her voice grew serious. "But, Matt, you be careful with that Jackson boy. Remember all those problems you had with his brother? That's a family you should probably stay away from."

Matt knew his mom was right. The Jacksons were an athletically talented bunch, but they weren't exactly the most functional family he had ever seen. He never saw them all together. In fact, come to think of it, Matt had never even seen their mother. Still, Ricky was different than either his older brother or his father. Matt liked him, even if he had almost gotten him into a ton of trouble in the game against Central.

"Are you coming to the game tomorrow?" Matt asked hopefully. "We're home to Churchill."

"Wouldn't miss it," his mom said. "You know what, I'm even starting to like football now that my son is playing the game."

Matt's mom dropped him at home before continuing off to her showing. Matt liked being alone in the house. He felt like watching TV, but instead he did the math homework he had put off the night before. Before going to bed, he flipped on the computer in his room. There was a new e-mail waiting for him. It was from Andrea.

Just wanted to say good luck against Churchill, she wrote. *See you at the game!*

It was late, but Matt knew Andrea would want to hear the news about Charlie. Charlie had helped her with her batting form when she was coming back from a serious leg injury during the previous softball season. The three of them had become close friends as a result.

Matt e-mailed her with the details. A few minutes later, he had another e-mail in his In Box. *That's awesome,* she wrote. *He never even mentioned he could kick.*

Come to think of it, Andrea was right. Charlie had never spoken about his own ability as an athlete. Matt had just assumed he didn't play sports because of the brace on his leg. As he drifted off to sleep he wondered what else Charlie was capable of doing.

Churchill was supposed to be an easy win for South Side, but that was on paper. Factoring in the loss of Nate Brown, whose injured ankle remained too swollen for him to play, and the fact that the Stingers were coming off a tough loss from the week before, Matt had a feeling this game was going to be a toss-up.

His premonition was right. On a clear, crisp autumn night, perfect for football, the Bulldogs and the Stingers turned in a barnburner in front of about five hundred fans. And with just two minutes left in the fourth quarter, the score was even at 10–10.

Matt was ecstatic about getting a chance to play almost every offensive down, and he felt he had performed well under the pressure of replacing Brown in the offense. He had caught five passes for about seventy-five yards, including one thirty-yard catch-and-run that had set up the Stingers' lone touchdown on a subsequent keeper by quarterback Kyle James.

Charlie's debut as the South Side kicker had been mixed. Although he hadn't shown any nerves during try-outs, the buildup to the Churchill game had seemingly caught up to him. Word had spread around school that the manager had won a job as the team's placekicker. Everybody was stopping Charlie in the halls and asking him about it, even the girls. As a result, he had been nervous tonight. He had missed his first field-goal attempt, a twenty-five-yarder in the first half, which was wide left. And he had barely made another of a similar distance early in the second half to put South Side up briefly.

With Brown out, Matt was playing a lot more—not only in the offensive sets but also on special teams. And with less than two minutes to go and the Stingers stalled on their own thirty-yard line, he remained on the field with the punt team.

Reggie Evans lofted the ball deep down the field toward Jimmy Flynn, the Bulldogs' star running back and return man. The punt was high enough that Matt had time to get downfield quickly and was nearly on top of Flynn when he caught the ball. Taking a chance, Matt left his feet on the dead run, hurling his body toward Flynn who was heading upfield. The two collided and the ball squirted loose, right into Matt's hands. He fell to the turf with the football under his body.

The referee whistled. Then he pointed in the direction of the Churchill goal line. Matt had caused a fumble, recovered the ball and put the Stingers in position to win in the dying seconds.

Coach Reynolds called a time-out, and the offense gathered around him. Kyle James was eye-to-eye with the coach, awaiting direction.

"Okay, same thing as last week, only this time we follow instructions," Coach Reynolds said, catching Matt's eye. "Kyle, I want you carrying the football. I don't want to risk passing it now. Keep it in the middle of the field. We'll call on Charlie if we need him."

Charlie Dougan was on the sidelines, pounding footballs into the practice net. He looked serious. Matt felt nervous for his friend. He kind of hoped it didn't come down to a field-goal attempt. Nobody needed that kind of pressure in his first game.

As usual, James ran the series exactly the way coach had called for it. On first down, he kept the ball and made it three yards up the middle. On second down, he gained four more. But just as Brown had the week before, James came up lame after being hit on the play, favoring his left knee. The confusion around his injury caused the

South Side students running the score clock to allow a few extra seconds to tick away. There were now just thirty seconds left in the game. Coach Reynolds called his final time-out.

James had been able to leave the field on his own power. But the coach took one look at his quarterback and made a decision. "We're going for the field goal now," he said.

Charlie snapped up his helmet and headed onto the field. For the second straight Friday, the Stingers were lining up to kick a field goal on the final play of the game with the outcome hanging in the balance. And now they were doing it with a rookie kicker. Matt put his arm on Charlie's shoulder. "It's just like batting practice," he said gently. Charlie stared at him blankly, then a crooked smile broke out across his face. Charlie had said exactly the same thing to him when he had gone up for a crucial at-bat during the base-ball season. "I hear you," he said.

Matt fielded the long snap cleanly from center Steve Donnelly and placed the ball nose down on the turf. He didn't see Charlie's motion as he addressed the kick but he felt the force of his right leg coming through the football, and he watched as it sailed cleanly through the uprights thirty yards away. It was a perfect kick. Charlie had delivered. Although there were still a few seconds left on the clock, South Side was up 13–10. Charlie had done it.

The Stingers' bench was going crazy. The players mobbed Charlie as he trotted off the field, slapping him on the helmet and shoulder pads and chest-bumping him. Watching the scene unfold, Matt felt good for Charlie.

He didn't have long to soak up the moment, however. Seconds later, Matt was back out on the field for the kickoff. Churchill had one more play in which to get back in the game. But there would be no miracle finish to this one. Charlie booted a solid kick to the five-yard line, and Jimmy Flynn was nailed at his own ten-yard line by Reggie Evans. The game was over.

chapter thirteen

Matt pulled off his football equipment, showered and dressed quickly. South Side had won the game in a terrific finish, but he wasn't feeling nearly as relaxed and happy as his teammates. In fact he was downright nervous.

After the last football game, Matt's father had said he'd like to meet some of his friends from the team. Matt had guessed it would be okay and hadn't thought too much more about it. But his dad had phoned a couple of nights later, offering to take him and some buddies out for burgers following the Churchill game. His mom had seemed okay with it, so Matt had agreed. But now he was nervous, and he wasn't sure exactly why.

Matt had invited Phil and Charlie to join him and his dad for the dinner at O'Regans, a local burger place not far from the school. So after Charlie had finished dressing and receiving the umpteenth round of congratulations from everyone in the dressing room, he joined Matt and Phil at the door. "Let's go," he said, smiling. "I'm starving."

Outside they spotted Matt's father, parked along Anderson, across from the school. His dad climbed out of the driver's seat.

"Hey, guys," he said, extending his large hand first to Phil and then to Charlie. "I'm Matt's dad."

"This is Phil and this is Charlie—they're two of my best friends," Matt said.

"Great to meet you both. You guys hungry?"

Phil and Charlie nodded. They all hopped into the SUV. It was quiet on the ride to the restaurant, until his father stuck a CD in the stereo and cranked up the volume. It was the Red Hot Chili Peppers. Until now, Matt had never considered the possibility that his dad might actually like decent modern music.

The four of them quickly loosened up over a dinner of cheeseburgers, fries and chocolate shakes and plenty of talk about football. After a physical game like the one against Churchill in the crisp autumn air, the food tasted awfully good. "That was a great game tonight," Matt's dad said. "And a terrific clutch kick, Charlie."

"Not bad for his first game ever," Matt piped up proudly.

His dad looked confused. Matt filled him in on what had happened that week with Ricky Jackson being suspended and the coach having to audition kickers to find a replacement.

"Sounds like your team has been through its share of drama already," his father said.

They all laughed. Little did they know, however, that the drama for the South Side Stingers was only beginning.

The next morning, Matt awoke early and headed for the front door. As usual, he would grab the *Post*, line up a big breakfast at the kitchen eating bar and devour the Sports section from front to back. During the school week, there wasn't quite as much time, but on the weekend he could slow down and catch up on all the news he had missed.

He didn't get far this time, however. In fact, the article running down the side of the second page of the *Post* Sports section almost made him choke on his Corn Flakes.

Frustrated football father files lawsuit, read the headline.

The father of an outstanding high school football prospect has launched legal action against South Side Middle School and its head football coach, Rick Reynolds, the story began.

Frank Jackson, whose son Ricky was suspended by the South Side coach this week, has filed a lawsuit contending that the boy was discriminated against and that his future as a football player has been diminished due to the suspension.

In the meantime, Jackson has obtained an injunction order from the Third District Court, compelling South Side to reinstate Ricky Jackson until the case can be heard.

Frank Jackson would not comment on the suit for the Post, *referring all questions to his lawyer. But his youngest son is already well-known in football circles after winning the regional Pass, Punt and Kick competition last year as a sixth-grader. Ricky Jackson is considered a can't-miss high school starting quarterback in the near future, and many are already tabbing him as a college prospect, following in the footsteps of his father who was an NCAA standout during the 1970s.*

Coach Reynolds was unavailable for comment. But a source close to the team told the Post *that the younger Jackson was benched recently after ignoring his coach's instructions during two consecutive games and allegedly taking hand signals from his father in the bleachers.*

Matt could hardly believe what he was reading. A lawsuit? Wasn't this going too far? It was only middle school, after all. Jackson's dad was pushy and intense, but this seemed over the top, even for him.

The story filled in some blanks for Matt, though. Now he understood why Ricky had changed that play at the end of the Central game. His dad must have still been signaling him from the sidelines. Even though Matt knew it was wrong not to listen to the coach's orders, he wasn't sure he'd be able say no to Frank Jackson, especially if he had to live with the man afterward.

Matt quickly finished his breakfast. He could hardly wait for Phil, Jake and Amar to show up for their usual Saturday morning hoops game at Anderson Park. He was bursting with the news of the lawsuit.

Phil was first at his door. "Can you believe

that story in the *Post*?" he said as he stepped inside. "I mean, I knew Jackson's old man was a jerk but this is unreal."

Matt nodded. "I feel sorry for the kid," he said. "Can you imagine living with that guy?"

"For sure," Phil said. "And I heard he doesn't have a mom around, either. She died of cancer or something when Ricky was young."

Matt hadn't realized that. It must be even worse than he imagined for Ricky, living in a house with only Grant and their obnoxious father around.

Jake and Amar were soon at the door. They hadn't heard the news. They were both shocked.

"Whoa, you football guys take things seriously," Jake joked. "Man, that Jackson family is messed up."

Matt had to agree. He wondered how Coach Reynolds was going to handle the court's decision. More importantly, he wondered how Ricky's situation was going to affect the mood of the South Side team. Things had been going well for the Stingers, but something like this had the potential to divide the locker room.

After several games of two-on-two at Anderson, Matt headed home. He had planned to use the afternoon to rake the leaves off the lawn and then mow the grass for what he hoped would be the final time until the spring.

He was just changing into some old work clothes when the phone rang. It was Charlie Dougan.

"Hey, Matt," he said. "Did you read the story in the *Post*?"

Naturally, Charlie had read it. Matt imagined that everybody on the football team knew by now.

"I guess that's it for me," Charlie said. He sounded tired.

"What do you mean?" Matt asked, before realizing what Charlie meant. Of course, if Jackson was coming back, he'd expect to be the team's placekicker again too.

"It's going to be tough to give back the uniform," Charlie said.

"You don't know that's what Coach will do," Matt said. "I think you're a better kicker than Jackson, anyway."

"Thanks," Charlie said. "I'm going to talk to Coach first thing Monday morning."

Matt was worried after he hung up the phone. Charlie had been so happy after earning a spot on the team and kicking the winning field goal against Churchill. It would be a shame if he now had to go back to being a manager. At the same time, Matt knew what Jackson's dad was like. The word *gimp* kept floating around in his mind as he finished his weekend chores.

chapter fourteen

The tension was obvious as the team gathered around Coach Reynolds before practice on Monday afternoon. Coach would normally follow up on the previous Friday's game and set the tone for the coming week with a few words each Monday, but this was different.

He cleared his throat. "I assume most of you guys can read," he said, smiling a little awkwardly. "So you'll already know about the story in the paper this weekend."

Heads nodded all around. A few players turned to glance at Ricky, who was suited up for practice and standing near the back of the group.

"I'm only going to address this issue once," the coach said sternly, his gaze meeting individuals' eyes in the group. "I don't want to hear about that subject around practice, or in games, or anywhere near this team. To me that whole issue is separate from football. You guys just worry about the game, and I'll worry about that stuff."

Matt wondered how Ricky would fit into the whole *let's-just-be-normal* theme. He knew how self-conscious he would be if he was in Jackson's shoes. But Coach Reynolds hadn't mentioned Ricky by name or gone into any specifics.

"Now, let's get to work," the coach said. "We've got Mandela on the road on Friday. If we win, we've still got a shot at the playoffs. If not, well, there's always next year."

Coach Reynolds was true to his word. He didn't mention the lawsuit and, as usual, he ran practice crisply and efficiently. The only difference Matt could detect was that Ricky was suddenly now taking equal reps at quarterback along with Keith Vickers. And unfortunately for the Stingers, starting quarterback Kyle James was still sidelined with the knee injury he had suffered against Churchill.

Matt quickly realized that the coach was simply following court orders. He had been directed by a judge to reinstate Ricky Jackson, and that meant that Jackson was once again the team's backup quarterback. The injury to Kyle James meant Jackson might even be the starter against the Mandela Lions this Friday.

Jackson didn't look particularly comfortable during practice, however. His throws were wobbly, he bobbled a few snaps and he seemed a step slower than usual. He wasn't moving with anywhere near the confidence Matt had admired in him since football workouts began back in August.

Ricky wasn't alone at practice. His father leaned over the chain-link fence for the entire session, carefully watching everything that was going on. Beside him stood a man in a dark suit, taking notes.

"Kicking team!" yelled Coach Reynolds toward the end of practice. "Let's get out there in field-goal formation."

As Matt joined the rest of the kicking team, he noticed both Charlie and Ricky moving out to the middle of the field. Dougan sprinted confidently to the huddle, while Jackson jogged slowly, looking toward the sidelines where his father stood, motioning for his son to hurry up.

"Okay, you guys split the reps," Coach Reynolds said, eyeing Dougan and Jackson.

Matt was happy to hear this. At least Coach wasn't dumping Charlie just because Ricky's suspension had been lifted.

Matt held for the two kickers as they took turns booting the ball, at distances increasing in range from fifteen to thirty-five yards. Charlie was stroking the ball nicely, but so was Jackson. At the end of the session, the two kickers had essentially competed to a draw. "Nice work, fellas," the coach said.

Charlie grinned and offered a hand to Ricky, who slapped it. It was nice to see the two of them being friendly, Matt thought.

"That's it for today," Coach Reynolds said. "Back at it tomorrow afternoon at four o'clock."

The coach headed to the locker room, with Matt, Charlie and a few of the other players several steps behind him. As he passed Frank Jackson and the man in the dark suit, Coach Reynolds did not acknowledge their presence.

It was chili for dinner that night. It was one of Matt's favorite meals, maybe not Mom's fanciest dish, but one that always hit the spot. He dug into his large, steaming bowl with gusto. Football made him hungry.

"So, Matt," his mother said. "I hear there's quite a controversy around the team."

Matt nodded. "It's pretty messed up," he said. "Ricky's dad is suing the coach. Ricky's back on the team, and poor Charlie's caught in the middle."

"I feel sorry for Charlie," his mom said. "That boy deserves to be kicking for South Side."

"Yeah, me too," Matt said. "But I kinda feel bad for Ricky too. I can't imagine living with a jerk like that for a parent."

Mom frowned. "Matt, you shouldn't talk like that about somebody's dad," she said. "Then again, you're probably right. Getting a lawyer seems to be an awfully extreme step to take."

"Mom, if I was benched for some reason you didn't think was fair, would you get a lawyer and sue the coach?" Matt asked.

It had been a serious question, but his mother just laughed. "I can barely afford regular briefs for you, kiddo, never mind legal ones."

chapter fifteen

It was not a normal week at South Side football practice. Other media had followed up on the *Post's* report, and a couple of television crews had even come to the field during practice to try to speak with players about the lawsuit. Matt realized that their interest had nothing to do with middle-school football—the reporters didn't care about that—but a story about a parent suing a coach and leaving a whole team of teenagers caught in the middle was of interest to just about everybody.

Coach Reynolds had strictly prohibited his players from talking to the TV crews, however. So mostly they just filmed bits of practice footage and talked to the few parents who would speak with them. Matt had watched a couple of the reports but hadn't learned much more than he already knew.

By game time Friday, the focus on the lawsuit had died down and everybody was concentrating on the game. South Side was 2–1 so far this season and needed to beat Mandela to have a shot at the conference title. Both Central and Churchill were 3–1 after their games this week, and they played each other in their regular-season finale. One of those teams would finish 4–1. The only hope for the Stingers of advancing would be for them to also finish at 4–1 and that Churchill beat top-ranked Central at the end of the season.

The team dressed and boarded two long yellow school buses for the thirty-minute ride across town to the affluent northern suburb where Mandela Middle School was located. It was the newest school in the district, named after the former South African leader, and although its football program had only been running for three years, the Lions were already a pretty decent squad. They weren't as good as Churchill or Central, but Matt knew they would be tough at home.

"Okay, guys," Coach Reynolds said, standing in the middle of the spacious visitor's locker room. "I don't have to tell you that this is a huge game. Your season is on the line tonight, and I want you all to play like it."

Matt could feel the urgency in the room. His own adrenaline was pumping. He wanted to get out there and knock down the entire Mandela offensive line all by himself.

Coach motioned to Charlie, who was sitting across the locker room in full gear. Charlie followed the coach into the hallway. The door closed.

Moments later, the coach emerged. Charlie was trailing. Matt couldn't tell by the look on his face what had happened. But Matt knew it probably wasn't good news.

He was right. As the Stingers' kickoff team lined up at midfield to start the game against Mandela, Ricky Jackson was the one getting set to boot. Coach Reynolds had obviously decided he had no choice but to follow the court injunction and pull Charlie for Ricky. Staring back at the sidelines at Charlie, Matt felt bad.

Despite his shaky start in practice and the pressure from the lawsuit, Ricky Jackson got off to a good start. His opening kickoff sailed over the heads of the return team and put the Lions in poor field position. And when South

Side got the ball back on a punt, Ricky engineered an efficient six-play touchdown drive, hitting Nate on a down-and-out pattern in the right corner of the end zone.

But Mandela quarterback Toby Renton, an eighth-grader with a strong left arm, recovered from his sluggish start to catch fire as the game progressed. By the end of the third quarter, Renton had thrown three touchdown passes and Mandela had worked its way into a 21–21 tie.

With Nate back in the lineup, Matt wasn't getting much playing time. He hadn't been out to hold for a field goal, either, since South Side had yet to attempt one. But Matt was still enjoying the game. Who wouldn't? These were two well-matched football teams, playing an important contest. Each side was performing well under the pressure.

Midway through the fourth quarter, Ricky busted loose on a quarterback sneak from the South Side fifty-yard line. He broke two tackles, and then he turned it up another gear, outrunning three more Lion defenders to the goal line. Ricky had scored the go-ahead touchdown with only eight minutes left.

But Mandela roared back. Toby Renton put

together the game's most impressive drive, mixing his left-handed spirals with deft handoffs to fullback Charles Maxwell, to string together a sixty-yard march and tie things up with four and a half minutes left.

From there the teams exchanged the ball twice, with neither mounting any offense. With fifty seconds remaining, Mandela was forced to punt from its own thirty-five. Matt and Reggie Evans waited downfield for the kick to arrive.

The ball shot off the Mandela punter's foot and rocketed high toward Matt, who was standing at his own thirty. His legs were already turning upfield as he caught the ball on the dead run and headed up the sidelines. His running catch seemed to take Mandela by surprise, and he broke through for an impressive thirty-five-yard return. With thirty seconds remaining, Coach Reynolds called an urgent time-out.

The South Side players gathered around Coach Reynolds on the sidelines, Ricky almost nose-to-nose with him.

"Here's what I want you to do," the coach said to Ricky. "Keep the ball in the middle of the field. If the ten-yard buttonhook to Nate is there, take it. Otherwise, Jackson, just keep it on the ground. We've got just one play to get within field-goal range. And we've got one more time-out. Make sure you use it."

Everybody nodded and the Stingers cheered. The offense then huddled around the ball. "Buttonhook to Nate, on three, okay?" Jackson said. "If it's not there, I'm keeping."

The Stingers went into their formation with beefy Pete Cowan back to protect Jackson in the pocket. On the snap of the ball, Nate ran straight out and curled quickly in the middle. Ricky delivered the ball on a tight hard spiral. Nate gobbled the ball into his arms. It was a first down on the Mandela twenty-five.

"Time-out!" Ricky yelled.

The players once again joined Coach Reynolds on the sidelines. "Nice work, Jackson," he said. "Just like we called it. Now, how about kicking us a field goal?"

Ricky shook his head slowly. He removed his helmet. "I think Charlie should kick this one, Coach," he said. "He's way more accurate than I am. And he deserves it."

"Dougan!" the coach yelled. "You ready?"

Charlie, at the back of the huddle, nodded. Matt pulled on his helmet. He would be holding for Charlie on this kick, the second game-winner in as many weeks for the former manager. As they headed out to the field, Matt asked Charlie, "You okay?"

"I'm better than okay," Dougan responded calmly. "I'm ready to win this thing."

The snap came back to Matt on the count of two. He spun the football into position just as Charlie drove his right foot through the leather. The kick barely cleared the outstretched arms of Mandela's Charles Maxwell, who had catapulted over the line in an attempt to block it.

But nobody was blocking this kick. True to his word, Charlie had booted it through the uprights from nearly thirty-five yards. The ball cleared its target by more than ten feet. South Side had won. The Stingers' playoff hopes were still alive.

Everybody was happy as they headed back toward the two yellow school buses. Everybody on the team, that is. One look at Frank Jackson told Matt that Ricky's dad was fuming once again.

As the players approached their buses, Mr. Jackson strode quickly toward them. He didn't say a word to Ricky but grabbed him roughly by the arm and quickly led him away to the parking lot.

Sitting on the bus, Matt wondered why Jackson's dad had been so angry. South Side had won, and Ricky had clearly been the team's best player. It had been his best game as a middle-school football player by far. Matt didn't get it.

As he waited for the bus to head out of the Mandela parking lot, Matt noticed Coach Reynolds and Frank Jackson facing each other some distance from the bus. It didn't look like a pleasant conversation.

chapter sixteen

Monday morning came too soon for Matt. For several days, he had put off studying for his Spanish midterm. He had cracked the main textbook for a few minutes over the weekend but had been sidetracked by pickup hoops, an NFL game Sunday and an unexpected visit from Mark, who drove down from Eton for dinner.

This morning, Matt had got up at 6:00 AM so he could get to school an hour early, grab the supplemental Spanish textbook from his locker and squeeze in some last-minute studying. Matt guessed he'd be the only one at South Side at seven in the morning, but he was wrong. As he swung through the front doors he saw Ricky Jackson, searching for something in his locker across the hall.

"Hey, Rick," Matt yelled. Nothing. Jackson didn't turn around. He didn't respond at all.

Matt crossed the hallway. Then he noticed Jackson was wearing the white buds of an iPod in his ears. The music was probably too loud. Matt tapped him on the shoulder.

Startled, Jackson spun around. Matt was shocked. The skin around Ricky's left eye was swollen and badly bruised. And the left edge of his nose was an ugly mix of dark purple and black. It looked like he had taken quite a beating.

"What happened to you, man?" Matt asked. "Get run over by a train?"

Jackson pulled the earphones out. "What?" he said.

"What happened?" Matt repeated. "To your face?"

Jackson turned back to his locker. "Nothing, man," he said. "It's nothing...I just tripped."

Matt wasn't buying it. Tripped? Nobody looked like that after a trip. Somebody had taken a round out of Ricky Jackson.

"Ricky, I'm not stupid," Matt said. "What happened?"

"Don't worry about it," the boy said. "It's my business."

Matt didn't know where his next comment came from. It just spilled out. "Did your dad do this?"

Jackson wheeled around. His dark eyes were watering and he was shaking. "Look, man, you don't know anything, okay?"

"What's up?" Matt said. "What's going on?"

"You wouldn't understand," Ricky said, slumping down beside his locker. He was crying now and his shoulders were heaving. Matt had never seen him like this before. Come to think of it, Matt had never seen any kid like this before.

"My dad…He just wants me to do so well. He wants everything to be just right," Jackson said. The tears were streaming down his face now. "It's not his fault."

"What's not his fault?" Matt said.

"He doesn't mean it," Ricky said. "He just can't help it."

Matt suddenly realized what Jackson was telling him. This was heavier than anything he had ever encountered with any of his friends. Just as Matt had guessed, Jackson's dad had done this to him. Matt couldn't imagine his parents doing anything like this. Ever. Even though he hadn't always respected his own father for leaving when he was just a toddler, he was sure his dad would never physically hurt him.

"You've gotta tell someone," Matt said. "This isn't right."

"I can't," Ricky said, sobbing. "He's my dad."

Matt was undaunted. "Look," he said, "your face is pretty messed up. Teachers are going to wonder what's happened. So is every kid at school. Why don't we go see Ms. Dawson? She's cool. She'll know what to do."

Ricky just stared straight ahead.

"If you don't tell someone, I will," Matt said.

Ricky glanced at Matt as if he was mulling over the idea. Finally he nodded his head. "Okay," he said wearily.

It was only 7:30 AM, but the lights were already on in Ms. Dawson's room. Matt knew nobody else would be in there at this time of day. Ricky would be able to talk to her alone.

Ms. Dawson was sitting at her desk, leaning over some marking, deep in concentration. Matt had to knock on the classroom door to get her attention. She looked up from her work. "Matt," she said warmly, her hazel eyes lighting up.

"What are you doing here so early? Advisory's not for another hour, kid."

Matt stepped aside and ushered Ricky Jackson into the room. "Ricky needs to talk to you, Ms. Dawson," he said. "It's pretty important."

The teacher took one look at Ricky's swollen eye and bruised face and walked quickly toward him. She remained calm, but Matt could tell she was concerned.

"Matt, can you give Ricky and me some privacy?" Ms. Dawson said. "And thank you for coming to see me. You're a good friend."

Matt blushed. He left Ricky and Ms. Dawson standing there in the classroom beside her desk. Jackson was still crying softly.

Matt hoped he had done the right thing. But Ricky was obviously hurt and upset. What else was there to do? Normally a guy could talk to his parents in a situation like this. But that obviously wasn't an option.

Matt thought about Ricky's badly bruised face all day. He didn't see him in the halls, and Ricky was missing from practice.

"Okay, boys," the coach said, during the Monday afternoon briefing. "We're down to the final week and we're still alive. That's a tribute to you guys. You've shown a lot of guts over the last couple of weeks. Now, we've got one game left this Friday against Manning. Beat those guys and we're still in the hunt. I know you guys can do it."

The players roared in agreement. The pace of practice was quicker than usual for a Monday. As the season wound down, the intensity level had steadily cranked up every week. Matt was sure the Stingers would be ready for Manning come Friday.

Matt was exhausted as practice came to an end at 5:30 PM. He was looking forward to just heading home and flopping down on the couch. There was no homework to do tonight, and he could afford to rest. It had been a long day.

Phil's parents had picked him up after practice to go out for dinner, so Matt was alone as he headed home. Half a block along Anderson Crescent he heard somebody calling his name.

It was Ricky Jackson. He was running to catch up. Matt stopped and waited. "Hey, Rick," he said.

"Hey," replied Jackson. "I tried to find you outside the locker room, but you were already gone."

Jackson was wearing a bandage across his left eyebrow and another one underneath his eye.

"The nurse had a look at me," he said, pointing to his face. "The social worker came around too," Ricky continued. "I just wanted to tell you. They're going to put me and Grant in another home for a while."

Matt was stunned. "Oh, man, Ricky, I'm sorry," he said. "I didn't mean to mess things up for you guys."

"It's okay," Jackson said quietly. "I mean, it's not the first time the social worker has talked to me and my brother. And it's not the first time he's hit me."

"You mean your dad?" Matt asked.

Jackson nodded. "He's always mad. I mean, I think he's trying to do what's best for us, but it never works out. Then he gets angry. And when he gets like that, you can't talk to him."

"Lately, it's been crazy," Ricky continued. "Him and Grant went at it twice last week. After Grant found out that he beat me up, they went at it again. I mean, he's my dad and everything, but it's too weird. And when he's like that, I hate him."

The words were spilling out of Ricky Jackson now. Matt felt sorry for him. But he also admired anybody who could survive being put in such a horrible situation.

"Bet your old man isn't like that," Jackson said.

"No," Matt said. "I mean, I don't know him that well, but I don't think so."

"What do you mean, you don't know him?" Ricky asked.

Matt explained that his dad had left home when Matt was three years old and had shown up again only a few weeks ago. Even though it was a new relationship with his dad, Matt realized that, compared to Jackson, he had it easy.

"I guess both our families are screwed up," Ricky said, laughing.

Matt laughed too. "Guess so," he said.

Matt suddenly had an idea. His mom was making dinner right now. She probably wouldn't mind having an unexpected guest. "Hey, Rick, do you want to come over for supper?" he said.

Jackson smiled. "I'd love to, man, but I can't. The social worker is at the school waiting for me. I just wanted to talk to you before she took me to the house where Grant and I will be staying."

"Okay, then," Matt said. "Some other time."

"For sure," Jackson said as he headed back toward the school. "And thanks."

chapter seventeen

As Matt headed home, his head was spinning. What Ricky had just told him blew his mind. On the one hand, he was happy his friend was going to a safe home that night, but he also felt partially responsible for Ricky's family being split up.

He was still mulling things over during supper. His mom called him on it after just a few minutes.

"Matt," she said, "what's up with you tonight? You've hardly said a thing and you don't seem that hungry. Are you okay?"

"Yeah," Matt sighed. "I mean, no. I'm kind of wondering if something I did today was the right thing."

He told his mom everything.

"I know you told me to stay away from Ricky," Matt said. "But he was messed up. I didn't know what to do. Maybe I should have just minded my own business."

She looked him in the eye. "What you did," she said, "was wonderful. I'm so proud that you tried to help that boy out."

"But did I really help him?" Matt wondered. "I mean, he's in a foster home now. His family is split up. His mother was already gone. Now he's lost his dad too. At least for a while."

"It sounds like his dad has some issues to work through," Mom said. "And of course you helped him. And Grant too."

Matt thought about it. He had actually helped Grant Jackson? That was hard to believe. Ricky's older brother had been constantly in Matt's face during the seventh grade, trying to pick fights with him and causing trouble. But now Matt had a little more insight into why Grant was the way he was.

"I tell you what, Mom," he said. "It makes me realize how lucky I am."

She reached across the table and hugged him. "I'm pretty lucky myself," she whispered softly.

After clearing the table, Matt was just getting

his coat on to take out the garbage when the phone rang. "It's for you, Matt," his mother called from the living room.

He picked up the telephone in the kitchen. It was Charlie.

"Hey, Matt, I just heard about Ricky," Charlie said. "I knew his old man was nuts, but that's pretty scary."

"Yeah, it is," Matt said. "The kid was pretty messed up."

"I bet I know why," Charlie said. "As he was pulling Ricky into the car, I heard his dad say that Ricky should have been the one kicking that field goal against Mandela. He said no gimp should be able to beat his kid out of a kicking job."

Matt was silent. The dead air was awkward.

"He was talking about me," Charlie said.

"That's pretty ignorant," Matt replied. "I'm sure that's not how Ricky feels."

"Ricky's a good guy," Charlie said. "I mean, he was the one who told Coach that I should be kicking. I feel kind of responsible for him getting beaten up."

"Hey, Charlie," Matt said, "it wasn't your fault. It wasn't Ricky's fault. His dad has got problems. I feel sorry for the kid."

"Yeah," said Charlie.

"And besides," Matt added, "Ricky was right."

"What do you mean?"

"You were the best choice to make that kick."

"Thanks, man," Charlie said. "See you at school."

After getting off the phone with Charlie and taking out the trash, Matt realized how tired he was. He headed up to his bedroom. But before turning in, he clicked on his computer. He had another e-mail from Andrea.

Heard what you did today, she wrote. *Matt, that was great of you to help Ricky. Especially after all the problems you have had with Grant.*

Just one more thing to add to my long list of reasons: "Why I like Matt Hill," Luv, Andrea.

Andrea's words made Matt feel warm inside. As he crawled into bed and turned out the light, he thought back to how crazily the day had started. But at least now, things all seemed to be going in the right direction.

Tuesday was a pretty normal school day compared to the way the week had begun. Matt walked to South Side with Jake and Phil, as usual. He talked to Amar before advisory and then had lunch with Andrea and a couple of her friends in the main foyer of the school. Between periods in the afternoon, he ran into Ricky. His face was already looking a lot better. Ricky nodded at him and smiled. But both of them had to hurry to a class in the opposite direction.

Practice was intense that afternoon. Kyle James seemed to be healthy and was back on the field and Nate Brown was running full steam. Matt and Ricky spent much of the session watching from the sidelines as the two senior starters took most of the reps.

"Okay, that's it," Coach Reynolds yelled at five thirty. "Everybody hit the showers. We'll see you tomorrow."

Matt walked toward the locker room with Ricky, Kyle and Nate. Up ahead, a dark-haired figure in a leather jacket was coming toward them. It was Grant Jackson, Ricky's brother.

Matt tensed. Since Grant had moved on to South Side High School, Matt hadn't seen him at all. He wondered if Grant still had it in for him, especially considering the situation with Ricky.

Charlie and Phil suddenly caught up to Matt. It was just like them, he thought. They were getting his back in case there was going to be trouble.

"Hey, Hill," Grant said, "got a minute?"

Matt stopped. "Sure." Phil, Charlie and the rest of the players moved slowly on ahead. Only Grant, Ricky and Matt remained standing by the chain-link fence that lined the South Side field, the same fence Frank Jackson had leaned over for all those practice sessions.

"I heard what you did yesterday," Grant said.

"Yeah, well, I…," Matt began.

"I just wanted to say thanks," the elder Jackson continued. "Our dad is pretty screwed up. He wants everything to be perfect, and when it isn't he goes crazy. He's impossible to live with, and he's especially tough on Ricky. It's been that way ever since our mom died."

Matt didn't know how to respond. He would never have expected Grant to thank him for anything.

"Something had to change," Grant continued, looking down. "But it's not easy to tell anybody when something like that's going on. So thanks for taking Ricky to see that teacher."

Matt nodded. Grant turned to his brother. "Come on, Rick," he said. "We've got a bus to catch."

"Later, Hill," Grant said.

"Later," Matt replied. "See you tomorrow, Ricky."

Phil and Charlie were waiting inside the locker room, bursting to hear about what had happened with Grant Jackson. "Was he pissed?" said Phil.

"You guys didn't scrap, did you?" Charlie added.

"No," Matt said, "he was cool. He just wanted to say thanks for helping out Ricky."

Even as Matt delivered that news to his two dumbstruck friends, he still had trouble believing it himself.

chapter eighteen

The phone rang at seven thirty Friday morning. Nobody called that early unless it was an emergency. Matt picked up the phone by his bed.

"Hey, Matt." It was his father. "I thought you'd want to hear the news as early as possible."

"What news?" he said, yawning.

"The good news for the South Side Stingers," his dad replied. "Last night's score: Churchill twenty-one, Central twenty."

Matt felt his heart thumping faster. The Stingers had a chance that night to clinch the conference title and advance to the playoffs. All they had to do was beat Manning and they were in.

"That's awesome," he told his dad. "Are you coming to the game?"

"I'll be there."

Matt hung up. Although it was early, he bounded downstairs to the front porch to pick up the *Post*. A shot at the playoffs. What a great way to start off the day.

Word had spread quickly at school. By noon, red-and-white ribbons with the slogan *Beat Manning!* were being sold at the pep team stand. Posters showing a gigantic hornet stinging a hapless Minuteman ball carrier into submission were plastered in the hallways. There was a buzz across campus, and every player on the team could feel it.

Matt was just heading to the locker room after the final bell of the day when he passed Andrea in the hallway. She was dressed in her full maroon-and-white South Side soccer uniform with the long striped socks and black cleats. "We've got a game at Manning today," she said. "I won't be able to come to your game, but I wanted to say good luck."

"You too," Matt said.

Andrea hugged him. Standing on tiptoes, she kissed Matt on the cheek. "Bye," she said.

"See ya," Matt replied, his face flushing. He looked around as students passed them in the hallway.

Matt continued to the locker room, more excited than ever about the game and their chances of making the playoffs. He was a little disappointed Andrea couldn't be there to see the game, but his mom and dad were coming. The idea still seemed weird. For so long it had been just him and his mom.

The atmosphere was businesslike in the Stingers' locker room. The players prepared mostly in silence, as if they realized the magnitude of this game and wanted to get each detail exactly right. After shaking some of their jitters during warm-ups, the Stingers trotted back to the locker room for their pre-game talk from Coach Reynolds.

"Guys, I know that this has been an interesting season, to say the least," the coach began. "But what's impressed me the most is how you all have managed to concentrate on football and avoid the distractions.

"I'm proud of the way you've been able to do that. I'm proud of the way you've fought through all our injuries and the other adversity surrounding this team. Now we've got one game left. I know you'll give it everything you've got against Manning. And whatever happens, that's good enough for me."

The coach had his players meet in the center of the crowded locker room. Kyle James stretched out his left hand, and every Stinger did the same.

"Who are we?" James yelled.

"We're the Stingers!" came the massive response.

"Where are we going?" James barked.

"All the way!"

Matt was so pumped up he could have run right through the heavy metal door of the locker room. As the team broke through the gigantic paper hornet and onto the field, the overflow crowd of more than five hundred cheered. This was the kind of atmosphere he had imagined when he decided to go out for football back in the summer.

Manning won the coin toss and elected to receive the football first. That meant Matt was on the field to begin the game. Charlie sent the kickoff high down the left side where eighth-grade Manning return man Travis Green was waiting. Matt knew all about Green. He had been Manning's starting point guard in basketball as a seventh-grader the previous winter, but football was his best sport. Like Ricky, he had been tabbed as a can't-miss high-school star of the future, mostly because of his breakaway speed.

Matt sped downfield toward Green, trying to get a bead on the Manning ball carrier. But he didn't have a chance. The speedy Minuteman back caught the ball on the dead run and burst up the middle of the field, behind a wedge of blockers. Matt couldn't get anywhere close to Green. Reggie and Ron Evans both dove for the ball carrier but missed badly. He was already nearing midfield with only Charlie Dougan to beat now. Charlie lunged at Green and appeared to be on the verge of bringing him down. But the Manning runner shook loose of the tackle and scampered untouched the rest of the way into the end zone.

The game was seconds old, and Manning was already leading by a touchdown. But that wasn't the worst of it. Back at midfield, Charlie Dougan wasn't getting up. He lay crumpled on the ground, holding his right wrist and twisting in pain. Matt realized now that Charlie must have jammed the arm when he tried to tackle Green. No wonder he hadn't been able to bring him down.

Dr. Baker headed out onto the field. He checked Charlie's wrist and then looked back at the coach, shaking his head slowly. It was pretty obvious: Charlie was done for the day.

South Side was down not only a touchdown but also a kicker. And that was the way the game seemed to go for the Stingers. Although they were the superior team—Manning had gone 1–3 so far this season—South Side simply couldn't get anything going offensively. By halftime, it was still 7–0 for Manning.

"Listen guys," Coach Reynolds said in the locker room. "You played hard in that first half. Things didn't go your way. We'll turn that around in the next two quarters."

The Stingers managed to even the count midway through the third quarter when Kyle James found Nate Brown on a long fly pattern. But unfortunately for South Side, they missed the convert attempt, after Steve Donnelly sent a wild snap back to Matt, and Ricky Jackson was unable to get the kick away.

That left the Stingers trailing 7–6 heading into the final few minutes of the fourth quarter. Maybe South Side was pressing too hard, but nothing was going right. Passes from James to Brown that had been automatic all season were being dropped or were falling short. Meanwhile, Manning wasn't moving the ball, either. As the final minutes ticked off the clock, the game had degenerated into a punt-fest.

With two minutes left in the game—and possibly the Stingers' season—Manning was forced to punt from its own thirty-yard line. Kicker Kenny Forshaw got off a solid boot that sailed down the right sideline to Ronnie Evans, who was waiting underneath. Evans returned the punt to midfield. South Side had one last chance to pull out this win and extend its season.

The Stingers seemed poised to make the most of the opportunity too. On first down, James found Brown over the middle for a ten-yard gain. Then the quarterback kept and scrambled for another first down. South Side was now within field-goal range. And with just twenty-five seconds remaining, Coach Reynolds didn't want to take any chances. "Field-goal team!" he yelled.

Matt trotted onto the field along with Ricky Jackson. Jackson looked nervous. He hadn't kicked well this season. In fact he wouldn't even be taking this attempt if Charlie hadn't hurt his wrist earlier in the game. Matt knew he could use a confidence boost, particularly after everything that had gone on in his life during the last couple of days. "Like you can," Matt said to Ricky as they walked into the huddle. "Like you can."

Matt called for the ball on the count of two. But the snap from Steve Donnelly was wild once again. The ball bounced crazily in front of him as the South Side line struggled to hold back the fierce Manning rush. Matt was acting on instinct now. He scrambled forward, grabbing the football with both hands and looking behind him. Ricky Jackson was thinking the same thing. He moved quickly behind Matt, heading around the right end. Matt swept his hands up, lateraling the football to Ricky, who by now was on the dead run. He held his breath as Ricky headed toward the end zone.

The crowd roared, sensing a Stingers' score. But just two steps before the goal line, Jackson was blindsided by a flying Travis Green, who had come all the way from his linebacker spot on the left side of the field. Green laid his body into Ricky, bringing Jackson to the turf in a heap on the one yard line.

The final horn sounded. The game had ended, and South Side had failed to score. The Stingers' season was over.

Matt couldn't believe it. Neither could Ricky, who didn't get up, lying one agonizing yard short of a South Side victory. Matt ran over to his teammate, extended his right hand and helped him up. "Nice try, man," he said. "You almost made it."

As the two players turned toward the sidelines, Matt wondered how Coach Reynolds would react. He had been angry the last time Matt and Ricky had tried to score on what was supposed to be a field-goal attempt. Now, with the season on the line, it had happened again.

Coach Reynolds was motioning to Matt and Ricky as they walked off the field. Oh no, Matt thought. He's going to rip us right here, in front of everybody. This was going to be embarrassing.

The coach grabbed each of the players by the shoulder pads and brought their faces in toward his. "Boys," he said, "that was a heckuva play off a bad snap. You gave it your best shot. Like I said, that's always good enough for me. Nice going!"

The words soothed some of the hurt Matt felt over the sudden loss and the end of his first football season. He looked over at Jackson and smiled. "Next year," he said, eyeing the seventh-grade star. "We'll get 'em next year."

They walked together toward the corner of the field, where they joined up with Charlie, who by now had his right wrist wrapped in an ice bag. "Nice run, Ricky," Charlie said. "You almost won it for us."

Matt looked up into the stands. Most of the fans were still seated. He spotted his mom, talking with the Wongs. A section over, he saw his dad, who was waving madly. Matt waved back. As he looked at his father he was surprised to see another familiar face. It was Mark, his older brother, sitting beside their dad.

"I gotta go say hi to somebody," Matt said to Phil and Charlie. "I'll catch you guys in the locker room."

Matt walked toward the bleachers. Mark saw him coming and bounded down several stairs and to the railing that separated the field from the stands. "Nice game, bro," Mark said, shaking his hand. "You guys almost pulled it out."

"Thanks," Matt said. "I'm surprised to see you here. I didn't know you were coming."

"I wasn't planning to," Mark said, pausing for a second. "But dad phoned me this week. He said it was a big game for you and I should try to make it down…"

That's not what Matt had meant when he said he was surprised to see Mark there. He was simply surprised to see his brother sitting anywhere near their father.

"I talked to Mom about it," Mark said. "She said she didn't mind if I hung out with Dad a bit. She seems to have forgiven him for leaving. I guess if she can, I can too."

"That's cool," Matt said. "I mean, I'm glad."

"I'll catch you later," Mark said. "You should get to the locker room."

His brother was right. Coach Reynolds would want to say a few words to the team after such a tough loss. The coach didn't like his players hanging around on the field after the final whistle.

But as he headed back to join his teammates, losing the game was the farthest thing from Matt Hill's mind. Yes, his first middle-school football season was coming to a disappointing end but, glancing back at the stands, Matt sensed that a whole new chapter for him and his family was just beginning.

Jeff Rud was a sports writer and columnist at various newspapers in Western Canada for twenty years. He is now a political reporter for the Victoria *Times Colonist* and the author of eight sports-related books.